I Want to Know That

I Will Be Okay

Deirdre Sullivan is a writer and teacher from Galway. She has written seven acclaimed books for young adults, including *Savage Her Reply* (Little Island 2020), *Perfectly Preventable Deaths* (Hot Key Books 2019), and *Tangleweed and Brine* (Little Island 2017). She was the recipient of the CBI Book of the Year Award in 2018 and the An Post Irish Book Award for YA in 2020. Her short fiction has appeared in *Banshee*, *The Irish Times* and *The Dublin Review*. *I Want to Know That I Will Be Okay* is her first book for adults.

I Want to Know That
I Will Be Okay

Deirdre Sullivan

BANSHEE
PRESS

First published 2021 by
Banshee Press
www.bansheelit.com

Banshee Press gratefully acknowledges
the financial assistance of the Arts Council.

ISBN 978-0-9956550-7-2 (paperback)
ISBN 978-1-8383126-0-2 (hardback)

Versions of these stories previously appeared in the following: 'The
Mother' and 'Skein' in *The Dublin Review*; 'A Scream Away From
Someone' in *The Irish Times*; 'All That You Possess' in *The Penny
Dreadful*; 'The Bockety Woman', 'Black Spot' and 'The Host' in *Banshee*;
'Pearleen' in *The Galway Review*; 'Little Lives' in *Uncertainties* (Swan
River Press); 'Appointment' in *Autonomy* (New Binary Press)

Set in Palatino by Eimear Ryan
Cover design by Anna Morrison
Printed in Ireland by Walsh Colour Print

To Katie and Rebecca.

For bringing my Bonnie to me.

Contents

I Want to Know That
I Will Be Okay

The Mother

When Laoise was a little girl she hated to see any sort of stranger. Unfamiliar faces made her scared, particularly if they were hairy, or belonged to other children. She didn't cry: she pointed and she screamed. Her mother's face would tighten with embarrassment, and she would scoop the outraged Laoise up in her two big arms, and try to shush her.

Her friends had all got married in the same year. The five of them from school, one after another. She had been a bridesmaid at two of the weddings, and done a reading at another. She had stuffed cards with money, walked the shopping streets for clothes and shoes and clutch bags.

Small talk at these things was always awkward, but big talk wasn't much better, Laoise reckoned. People felt entitled to little bits of her. When Laoise was single, it was who she was seeing, was there anyone serious, and when it would be her turn. She thought about giving up trying to pass the strange tests that people set. Maybe buying a dog. Something golden, loving. A head to rub. A belly and soft eyes. The thing about a dog was that it loved you. That was just their nature. Humans wanted things. More things than love.

And then she met Jim. Are you moving in together? Do you think he will propose? Have you set a date?

Jim was a little older. They loved each other almost right away. The time was right, and love comes really quickly when you're grateful. A warm back and a kind voice – he proposed and then it was her turn. She made him shave his beard for the big day. It was something special, in the end. Her father proudly walking down the aisle. Jim neckless in his suit, but still, so charming. The sanctuary of that. *I'm there now*, Laoise thought. *Where people are. I'm there.*

And then it was babies. Have ye thought about it? Are ye trying? Mammy wanted grandkids, Dad dropped hints as well. You next. You next. You next. Jim didn't mind. He said he wasn't the type to let other people dictate the way he lived his life.

We married in a church and I wore white, Laoise thought. *You put a gold ring on my fourth left finger. That wasn't you. It was the weight of them. And also love.*

One by one, her friends filled up their happily married wombs with little babies. Laoise bought so many tiny outfits, signed so many cards. And meanwhile they tried, Laoise and Jim, but still the blood kept coming every month. It had always horrified her a little, the bleeding. It seemed so animal, like something that should not have to be borne. She had an iPad and an Orla Kiely bag with matching wallet. She shouldn't have to drip and hurt and stain. That's not what life should be. Not once you're married.

After a while they stopped officially trying, but she could see it written on his face when they made love: *Look how casual this is. How spontaneous. We're not trying but maybe it will happen. Just for us.* It made it hard to enjoy physical intimacy. She felt a bit like a toaster on the blink. He put the bread in, but no toast popped out. The element stayed cold and iron grey.

She began to resent him, with his shoulders and his golf clubs and his voice. When her friends met up they all had kids and she just had a womb that didn't work. Or maybe it did work, but not with Jim.

They hadn't been to the doctor. It was that thing of wanting kids, but not so much that you'd look for help from other people. It felt like something they should be able to do all by themselves, together. And they had time. Not lots of it, but some.

Jim said that if you adopted, you'd wait for years and not be sure exactly whose it was, or what could go wrong, genetically. Laoise thought of men with beards, of children who were cleverer than her, or very stupid. Who failed in ways they weren't supposed to fail. She felt the welling anger-fear from childhood. The urge to point her finger, raise her voice. She didn't want that difference in her life.

She took up Pilates, clean eating. Lost a stone and a half. After a while she stopped getting a period altogether. She didn't get her hopes up. She knew why. Jim wanted more sex, but her body was probably less able for it. The gym made her happy. There was a satisfaction in the work that had been done, and motivation for future sacrifices.

She never said no to Jim. She touched his body and made the sounds he liked. She imagined shrinking into the sheets sometimes, flattening into a paper doll and lying there, not having to do anything, please anyone. When she did that, and if she focused on it fully, there was a little joy that came along.

She never really thought about Jim's happiness. He ate his toast. He drank his tea. He told her about things. She listened. He went to matches, sometimes to the golf club. They booked weekends away and little holidays. She walked fifteen thousand steps every single day and sometimes he came walking with her. He made her laugh unexpectedly every now and then, in a way that other people couldn't. She'd roll her eyes and talk about him to her friends, or to people in the office, in the usual 'aren't men incompetent' sort of way. Half of being married was being fondly, publicly annoyed.

Their friends had a second round of babies. Laoise and Jim were godparents to one or two. Could take them to the zoo or babysit. Hand them back, all full of love and chips. It didn't make them sad, though Laoise could see how it could have done. If they were other people.

One day, Laoise arrived home from work, hung up her trench coat in the hall, and took her travel cup out of her Mulberry bag to rinse it. Jim was in the kitchen, perusing something intently: a catalogue? Jim liked catalogues. IKEA, Argos, Trailfinders. He'd pick them up and take them home. Choose what he would buy, where they could go. And then not buy anything, go anywhere.

'What's that?' she asked, scrubbing at the brown scum on the travel cup. You had to work at it or there'd be staining – ghosts of tea bags past. Some people let it build up, then used Milton. But the thought of drinking from something dirty bothered Laoise. She placed the bright white cup on the rack to dry, ready for the morning. Over her shoulder, she could see the awkwardness of Jim. Half slouched over, half turning towards her.

'Oh. Nothing.' Then he muttered, 'It's a bit mad.' His face was shifty, but his hands moved slowly, wanting her to look.

'Well, *I'm* a bit mad.' Laoise smiled, taking carrots out of the salad drawer and beginning to peel them. 'So you might as well tell me.'

'It's just this clinic.' Jim was wearing a polo shirt and jeans, sipping a flat white he'd bought from the new place down the road. He'd worked from home today. They had a coffee maker, but he liked the excuse to go for a little jaunt. He took a fifteen-minute break, and a twenty-five-minute one. He set a timer for them.

He held up the catalogue. There was a baby sloth on the cover, offering a hibiscus blossom to the photographer with a wet look of tenderness.

'Ahhh look,' Laoise said, putting down the peeler. 'Wait, is that the lads …'

'Yeah,' said Jim, 'from the radio.'

They'd heard about it driving home from work one day, in different cars but listening to the same station. It was catching on. There were clients who were really happy. She'd see them in the parks with small raccoons, red pandas. The odd bear. You wouldn't really see the ones with mice or guinea pigs. For smaller ones you didn't need a leash, harness or buggy.

When they passed by, they sometimes met your eye and smiled. Like, 'Fucking judge me. I am happy.'

Laoise wasn't sure how she should feel. It wasn't normal. She knew that. But it made the world a bit more magical, like seeing a celebrity, or someone from the news but in real life. A slow loris with eyes as wide as saucers. A lemur peering out from a pink fleece. Small soft things were pretty. Hard to judge. And they wouldn't care about it if you did judge them, would they? Their brains weren't built that way. Could be a good thing.

'We haven't seen a sloth yet,' she said to Jim.

'No.'

His voice was low. 'I'd like to …'

Laoise cut across him. Her voice was high, a little too upbeat. 'We could take Ciarán to the zoo again. I mean, if you wanted to look at sloths. I know it's not the same thing, not exactly.' She wanted to finish speaking, but her mouth was full of words. It wouldn't stop. 'It's been a while since we went somewhere like that. A day out. We wouldn't even have to take him – Ciarán.'

'No,' Jim said. His eyes met hers. 'I mean' – and there was something threaded through his voice, an odd sort of energy – 'I mean I'd like to think about … like: this. I ordered it. The catalogue. Online. They don't include the full range or a price list on the website. Like wedding suppliers.' He rolled his eyes to heaven with a smile. Jim liked remembering the day they'd had. The work that they had done to make it happen. Laoise rolled hers back. She liked that too.

'Oh,' she said, and paused and took a breath. 'Let's have a look then.'

There was no harm in having a look. Listening to someone's opinion. Exploring your options. It was fine. Absolutely normal. To listen to your husband. Give him time. This was how you made a marriage work. Supporting each other. The carrots weren't cut yet, only peeled. But it was fine. This clearly mattered to him more than dinner.

'I've often thought,' Jim said, 'that a child is kind of … long-term.'

That had occurred to Laoise too. Seeing her friends so tired, bags growing under eyes and staying put.

'And we both love animals,' he said.

'But you can buy an animal,' Laoise pointed out. 'In a pet shop. Or from a breeder. Or rescue.' The calmness of her voice surprised her. She thought she should be more confused, upset. It should feel stranger than it did.

'It wouldn't be ours, though,' Jim said. 'This way it would be. And they say it's very safe. Almost safer than the normal way.'

'Really?' Laoise asked, flashing into labour, flesh and strain.

'Well, depending on what you go for, they can be much smaller than a baby. And we'd obviously be going private, so there's that higher level of care involved …'

Jim had thought this through, it seemed.

But, essentially, Laoise thought, in bed at night, as his breathing slowed and deepened, *it would be me. In a room. Giving birth to an animal. A freak show.* She closed her eyes and planed her fingers across the flatter layers of stomach, the fruit of all her work.

Herself and Jim had watched all of *Planet Earth* together several years ago. She hadn't noticed him getting broody then. Nature was cruel and devastating. Things were beautiful and complex and then got eaten.

She rolled towards Jim and took in his warmth. Breathed the smell of sweat and dust and sweet chilli crisps. Jim always snacked – he munched through everything when he was working. It was endearing, his lack of discipline. Laoise mentally listed all the things she had forbidden herself: milk, cream, cheese, butter, bread, pasta, chocolate, juices of all sorts, fancy crackers that looked healthy but were secretly one hundred calories a pop and then why would you? She never had anything more than a glass of wine when they were out – she'd sip it to be normal.

Laoise walked twenty thousand steps a day that week. Rang her friends and asked them for their problems, to distract her. She didn't mention hers, they didn't ask. The catalogue was there upon the table. She'd leaf through it. Looking at the pages he'd dog-eared. Big golden yokes, mainly. Jim liked dogs, just like Laoise. They loved you back.

She'd always thought that they were boring sorts of dog, the ones Jim liked: Labradors, retrievers. Loyal, companionable. Nothing wrong with that, but Laoise craved a little bit of work. A wizened peke, a snappy Pomeranian. Something that would not be friends with everyone. Just hers.

They sat and talked about it, in the evenings.

'Loyalty is important,' Jim said.

'I agree.' But Laoise didn't just want slavish loyalty. She wanted to earn it with love.

'I'd like it to be clever,' Jim said too.

'Not too clever, though. When we're at work all day, it would go mad.'

'We wouldn't leave it in the house alone, though,' Jim said. 'It wouldn't be a pet. We'd have to care a little more than that.'

Fair enough, Laoise thought. *We can sacrifice a holiday a year for expensive doggy day care.*

'What about a cocker spaniel?'

'They like a rural setting,' Jim said.

'Next door have one.'

'Yeah, a *pet*. But it probably isn't perfectly happy.'

'I suppose.' Her voice was soft towards him. They were so close, she felt the heat of skin against her mouth.

'I'd like our dog to be perfectly happy,' he said.

Our dog. It sounded nice. That night, when they had sex, it felt like love. Like two of them together in the bed, sharing a thing. She traced her fingers across his chest hair after, coming down. She stroked and stroked. It wasn't very soft.

That Friday, a man and a woman and their panda, Daisy, were on *The Late Late Show*. They watched it after dinner, sipping wine.

'We were thinking about having children, but humans aren't an endangered species ...' the man began.

The woman started ranting about the planet, but the host directed her back to the strange thing she'd let inside her womb.

Fair play to him, thought Laoise. *Knows to give the people what they want.*

The couple's message seemed to be: Don't judge us, but we are better than you and have got a certificate from a zoo to prove it.

It was a lovely piece of paper, had that old tea-stained sheen, and they'd gotten it framed. Dublin Zoo had committed to building a special enclosure for Daisy to live in when she was old enough to move out. The couple would be sad to see her go, but they were very keen on Daisy realizing her full potential.

'Parenting a different species requires a level of empathy that's not for everyone,' the man said, and the woman held his hand and nodded enthusiastically.

'They're not, like, *pets*. That's what people do not understand.'

The host adjusted his skinny tie and leaned in, in a calculatedly disarming manner. 'Anne-Marie, though ... you were reluctant at first, am I right?'

'I was, for sure. I was. When you think of giving birth to something, you wonder about the risks. The responsibility. It's hard to be a mother in the world.'

'It's true. We don't appreciate mothers enough. Let's take a moment to clap for all the mammies out there.'

The audience applauded.

'And,' the husband pointed out, 'the two of us – we don't really like people, and the world doesn't need more of them. And then there's this. We get to have the experience. And it's demanding. It is. But not as long-term.'

'And safe?'

'Oh, *very* safe.' Anne-Marie's eyes bulged as she said this. Her husband patted her knee. She was wearing a black-and-white sheath dress. Very on-brand.

The subject changed; another guest emerged.

Laoise looked at Jim. He looked at her.

'I don't want a bear,' she said. 'Any sort of bear. I mean, imagine.'

Jim rolled his eyes. 'I know. The notions.'

'Notions!'

They laughed together, and while they were getting ready for bed, toothbrush sticking out between his lips, he said to her: 'You choose the breed. I don't care. You know the ones I like, but whatever happens, I'll love it and you.'

And Laoise smiled. The next day, she made the appointment.

They went in for the pre-counselling – three sessions. They signed the forms.

The night before the procedure, Laoise whispered to Jim, 'Do you want to know, or do you want it to be a surprise?'

He grinned. 'Surprise.'

Then, the following morning, he said, 'I've reconsidered: tell me, tell me.'

'Are you sure?'

He smiled at her. His face looked very fat, collar buttoned right up to the top. 'I've never been more sure of anything.'

'I decided to go with a …' Laoise made a drum roll on the table. 'Lurcher.'

Jim welled up. 'For …'

'… your grandad,' Laoise finished. She was feeling quite emotional, looking at Jim's face. She hadn't seen him cry in years. It was nice. She'd always liked Jim's grandad, a grizzled, druidical man who would have made a very handsome dog.

'Hopefully it won't be a racist lurcher,' Jim joked.

'Arrah, stop. He was of his time.'

His fingers brushed the top of her belly. Laoise smiled at him.

'That's perfect, love,' he told her. 'You are perfect.'

He kissed her like it was their wedding day. With sweet relief.

Laoise closed her eyes and held her head snuggled against his chest. The feelings in them were so deep already. It would be a lot of pressure to put on a child. A puppy would be more equipped to bear that weight.

Lying there, thinking of the changes that were coming, she thought of getting the house ready. Of walks. Of the two of them together loving something else in perfect harmony. This was something she could give to Jim. He had looked at her with worship in his eyes and that sparked something deep inside the taut plane of her stomach. She knew it wouldn't be that way for long.

It didn't occur to her that after it was finished, her body would disgust him. That he would love the dog but hate the wife. That welcoming this spark would snuff out something. Other people's eyes would make him cold.

All in all, though, she did not regret it.

There are things that teach you who you are.

A Scream Away From Someone

During the Blitz, my uncle moved to London. He was a gay man and it wasn't easy for them here at the time. It probably isn't easy for them now. I wouldn't know. He was the only one I ever had any contact with.

My uncle was a tall, thin, soft-spoken man. He had a fondness for pale colours – dove grey, bone, that sort of thing. They blended better into a big city like London. People got away with things there that they couldn't in other places. That's still true.

He was an able-bodied man and he found work. He had been worried people over there would call him a coward for not fighting. He'd heard things from men who hadn't fought in the first one, soft feathers pressed into their hands like little knives, stabbing looks from patriotic women.

It was all right though, he was left alone to find his way. There was a calmness about him, a sort of peace. A blankety thing like him wouldn't do too well in combat and people sensed that and left well enough alone.

My uncle liked the night-time. It had been calmer and emptier than the day back home but here the night was different. The sky was different. Different shaped clouds and the stars were hard to make out in the distance.

15

Hauling bodies was what he worked at. Long after people had been rescued, brought to hospital, he'd trawl through what was left to find the dead.

I have very few memories of him. I was born when he was older still, long after the war had ended. Back in those days women had litters instead of families and my mother was the runt of hers. She had me at fifteen, and they sent her over there to live with him. Otherwise, she would have had to go into a home for the unmarried.

I never found out who my father was. 'A man,' she'd say, which wasn't very helpful. She knocked six months off my age when she moved home. And added in a husband. With TB. She modelled him on my uncle's friend. Not that he got TB and died. He didn't. But in the looks and personality of things. She needed someone who'd be in a photo she could show them. She didn't know a lot of other men.

I believed the lies she told for ages. About the husband, about where I came from. It was only later, safely married, that she started to let pieces of my early childhood spill out at me. Stories about my uncle and his friend. The life they had together. The friend had a wife as well as my uncle. But he'd had my uncle first and they would stay friends till one of them was dead.

They had an arrangement about that as well. If my uncle died first, his friend was to go to his funeral. But if the friend died first, my uncle was to avoid the service at all costs and mourn him privately in his own way. The friend loved the wife, you see. But like you'd love a sister. My mother often wondered if the wife knew. And – once my mother married – how she didn't.

My uncle had a two-bed apartment that he owned, and she stayed there till I was two or three. I was small. She cleaned the place for him and made him dinners. Told him when he had toothpaste in the corner of his mouth. For a man who took pride in his appearance, there was always a little bit of dishevelment about him. A little flaw. A tattered patch of furze he'd missed while shaving, a piece of lettuce stuck between his slightly bucked front teeth.

He would have liked the pair of us to stay, my mother told me. He never asked, nothing so direct, but he told her we would always be welcome, more than welcome, when she began to make her plans to leave. Which might have been politeness, but my mother was perceptive. She knew things about people instinctively. She hated my first husband, made him put the milk in his own tea.

My uncle's soft hands became callused and scarred from the cement and brick and wood and dusty plaster debris. By the time my mother lived with him, he wore leather gloves with soft wool lining when he left the house, and always carried hand cream. It had a very particular scent, something between Vicks VapoRub and cedar. I've smelled it since. Brought water to my eyes.

My uncle found babies roughly twice a week. Children were scarce – a lot of them had been sent to the country. The ones that were too loved stayed in London. Rarer than babies, but not uncommon. A lot of people want their children near them. My mother wanted me. She could have given me away but kept me close instead. I'm glad of that. A lot of women didn't get the choice.

My uncle would find photographs in frames or wallets, sometimes in the gutters or blowing through the streets like dirty leaves. He would always try to pair them with their owners. Leave them in nearby shops or post offices or with the police. He would return to ask if anyone had found them, and if not would take them home, file them away, leaving his address. We found boxes of them when we cleaned out his house. Pictures of his family and friends all mingled in. It was hard to tell the strangers from the blood.

The worst thing that ever happened to my uncle didn't seem that bad to me at first. I loved this story when I was a child, and so did my mother. She was still a child when she had me. She shouldn't have been let. I mean, she didn't know what sex even was until she had it. Even then. She said that once and when I asked her more her mouth got tight and she emptied a drawer full of keys and receipts and bits of string and cleaned it out and made it tidy.

I helped her, tying all the string together, winding it into a ball the size of my fist, still smaller then than hers. She was a big woman. Not fat, but tall and wide. She must have developed early. Women shaped like that so often do.

My uncle only told it to her once. The night before she left. They were sitting down on his uncomfortable sofa. He loved old furniture with wooden legs and velvety upholstery, and it always looked beautiful and felt horrible, especially on bare skin. She was all packed and ready to go back and he told her she didn't have to.

He was drinking a large glass of red wine. He called it that, 'a large glass of red wine', and she had a smaller one to sip. Her special one. She didn't like the taste, but she wanted to keep trying it because it looked so elegant. And they sat together on the uncomfortable furniture and she had me – at that stage a little sleeping toddler – in the box room and they sat together and they sipped and he told her a story.

Sifting through rubble is hard work and hauling corpses out is harder still. You keep a scarf over your nose so you don't breathe powder in and even so your handkerchief fills up with grey and black. After a while, you start to see pieces of people you know. Your father's nose on some-one else's face. Your mother's knuckles. The forehead of your schoolmaster. It's like a jigsaw that makes the wrong picture. Not the one that's on the box, but something only slightly like it. This is what my uncle told my mother and I do not disbelieve him.

He didn't want to work with his hands, he wanted to do brainwork and he got that later, translating texts. Before that though, the hours he had to keep were strange and irregular. You take what you can get when you're an immigrant. You do what you need to do to keep your head above water.

Some nights, there'd be very little to do; they'd wait around. And others, they could work into the morning, afternoon, until they couldn't move. He always hoped to find somebody living. Every now and then that happened. Once he found a nest of kittens in the stuffing of an old armchair. He kept one but it died before my mother lived with him. Probably for the best. Cats don't like babies. Noisy things, encroaching on their space.

One night, my uncle found a shoe, sticking out of the rubble. It was a soft, tan, leather shoe. He knew the sort. They came from Woolworths. He had seen them. They were more expensive than what he wore. This was in the days before the good job and the rich friend.

The building, or what had been a building, was in a good area. Leafy, white houses with steps up to them, and wide streets. Big houses for big people, my mother used to say. I think her mother said it before her. And the shoe was attached to a foot, which was attached to a leg and some-thing about the leg was quite unsettling. He couldn't put his finger quite on what. The angle or the shape. It bothered him that he did not know why he felt so awkward looking at it. Trepidation, or the birth of fear.

My uncle noticed things about people. He was observant, fond of music, art. A decent listener. Sensitive. You wouldn't put him rooting through the dirt for bits of people. But he got down to it. He did his best. With the Luftwaffe in the forefront of your mind, there wasn't a lot of time to be bothered by the job at hand. Finding little children, especially inside their mother's arms, would do it. Grown men were rare enough; a lot of them had gone to fight the war. My uncle pulled hard at the leg but the pieces of house would not dislodge and so he had to pick and pick for ages.

The men who found the bodies worked in pairs, two of them in the one place. Some people worked in tandem, digging and chatting. My uncle and the man he generally worked with would go to separate areas and tease a body out, only helping each other if absolutely necessary. My uncle was a quiet man, not much for chat unless he knew you. He found the women easier than men. He liked the gentle people. His workmate was a rough sort, with a fancy voice. My uncle reckoned he might have come from bigger people once. He never asked, the workmate never offered.

In the blitz-lit darkness, there were always scavengers around as well. If you asked them, they'd pretend that it had been their house but they were lying and you had to run them. They were only out for things to steal from other people's dead. Scum, my uncle called them.

It happened on a cold night, and my uncle's workmate (respiratory issues and flat feet) wanted to get back to his wife who'd had a baby. He called her 'the missus' and the words sounded strange on his posh tongue. There was grime all over them, not black grime like miners get but a matte white pallor. 'We looked like ghosts,' he told my mother. 'The skin and in the eyes.'

My uncle kept on digging. And digging. Soft wool trousers, charcoal grey. It's hard to tell in the dark, but they had a flashlight, and they looked charcoal grey. They felt expensive. My uncle pulled them back over the leg and smoothed them down. The body had been dead a while; it was stiff but pliable. Rigor mortis had been and gone. The building had been bombed the night before. Looking back, my uncle thought it strange, but at the time he didn't know enough to put a name on his unease.

Digging and digging. A slim, soft stomach covered by a waistcoat. Mother-of-pearl buttons. Thin and delicate. Tasteful. No jacket, in his shirtsleeves, rolled up. The arms were outstretched, and it took the length of torso to uncover them. The corpse, it seemed, was completely upside down, splayed unnaturally. It was peculiar.

My uncle didn't like it. His partner smoked and sighed, not offering to help while my uncle scrabbled at it with his two big paws. Pulled the arms out by the elbows, awkwardly.

Eventually, his workmate came to help haul the body out with him. It's hard to lift a man's weight by yourself. Men are heavy things. When I was little my mother told me to be careful of all men. Strangers and the ones I knew as well.

'If you are in a room beside a man,' she said, 'keep the door open, love. Always be a scream away from someone.'

When the body was stretched out, my uncle found himself examining it. It reminded him of someone, but he couldn't put his finger on who. He wiped the dust off the man's face with his sleeve. The small eyes, widely spaced, the high sharp cheekbones, the little port-wine stain upon the chin.

His workmate eyed the corpse, and said: 'It's you mate, only older.' The more my uncle stared, the more he saw the truth in that. It had his face, but didn't have his life. They lumped it on the stretcher, sent it on its way to a decent burial.

My uncle never found out who that man was. The one that sort of lived inside his body. Like townhouses, they look the same but you don't know what's inside until you peep. Condemned, my uncle thought, filching through the silk-lined empty pockets. There was no wallet. No man had lived inside that house, a neighbour told him later. Only spinsters, and their little niece. My mother always gave that girl my age, when she told the story. To make me feel a part of it, I think.

Not a scratch on him. Dust but not a scratch.

The story wasn't scary enough to stop me sleeping as a child, but still it gave a pleasant nervous feeling and she told it to me quite a few times. The ending never changed. Her brother sad, and staring at his wine and saying dully:

'When I look in the mirror, loveen, it isn't my face that I see. Not anymore. It's always his. Since that night. Never mine.'

I never really understood the horror of that until I was older and began to shy away from mirrors, taking better care of my skin but knowing it was quite a pointless endeavour. Sometimes I look at my own face and imagine it's a stranger far away. Someone I've discovered nearly dead. I wait for it to move and when it does, I get a sick little thrill. I've caught it out.

I lie awake sometimes, beside my husband, a scream away from no one. My two fled the nest as soon as possible.

And I think of my uncle. We visited him twice, after that. Once when I was ten, for a weekend. And again, at his funeral. His friend long gone, and no one in the chapel knew our names. My mother in her little suit beside me. Knees together, hands inside her lap, staring ahead.

I scanned the faces in the crowd and wondered if someone here was happening upon his own face and body at the end of someone else's life. I wondered if I screamed who would hear me, and how many would come and would they help at all or make things worse. I held my tongue and counted the words in the Lord's Prayer. Twice. The answers were completely different both times.

All That You Possess

His name is Pebbles, she tells you, and you smile and ask her more about him.

He is four hundred years old, she says, and I am three.

She is standing on the bed in panties and a little cotton vest, sticking out her tum at you and grinning.

Her birthday was a month ago and she is proud of being three, waiting for the half to grow on top of it.

What is Pebbles like? you ask her. She is yours and she is cute. Her name is Ella. Ella Bridget Lily.

She is different to you. She is full of everything.

Her little face.

Is he your friend? you ask, and she says no.

And then she says, I'm not sure what he is. He's nice sometimes. He wants to eat my toes. He is a squirrel.

Like the ones in the park?

Not like the ones in the park, she says. He is a different squirrel. He is bigger. Bigger than them. But not as big as me.

Ella stands on tiptoes on the bed. She comes up to your shoulder, thrilled with being big. You always hated it. The size of you, they'd say.

The size of you.

There's nobody like Pebbles, Ella tells you. He's the only one of what he is.

Now you are a woman and you have a daughter. So you eat your dinner. Never comment on your body's shape. You want her to be strong and proud and confident. You want the world to be her fruit to eat.

You tell him about Pebbles when he gets home. She's already sleeping in her bed. It has a rail so she does not fall out. She's scared of falling. It makes it harder to climb out as well, and sometimes you feel guilty about that. You don't want to trap her, but you're working on her not coming in between the two of you. She is a light sleeper. All it takes is just a little sound, the faintest car alarm, a door closed gently. She wakes and she gets cold and wants the plushy comfort of your body. But so does he. It's hard. It's hard now to be married, have a kid. That's two jobs by itself. Your heart is split.

He's a light sleeper too. They share that, the way their foreheads furrow, and impatience. When she comes in, he won't get back to sleep, and you won't either as he rolls and sighs. You do not tell him that you want her with you. Little love-stove pressed into your crook. You stroke her curly head, the brain you made. The brain you grew inside you. And she is unique. A small old soul. You and him had nothing to do with it, you think sometimes. She would have happened anyway. And if she wants a cuddle, so be it.

Soft touch, he calls you. Sometimes fondly. And you love him too, you do. You do. It's just … there is a rhythm to you and Ella. Something he can't grasp. It's easier to do it all yourself, and then resent him for it.

Ella is in the buggy with you the next time she starts talking about Pebbles, the four-hundred-year-old squirrel.

He wants to eat my toes at night. He *licks* them.

He does not, you say.

She tells you that he does. With his big red tongue. All sticky. Pebbles is a crazy guy, she says. A *crazy guy*.

She smiles. Where did she get that language from, you wonder? Crazy meaning funny. Meaning wild. You notice it when other people use it. You don't yourself. You haven't since you got out at nineteen. Anyone can wobble at nineteen, your mam said then, and you tell yourself still. Anyone can have a little wobble. And you're grand now. You are grand. And look at all you have. A lovely house. A lovely husband. Child.

The little angel, Mam sometimes calls her. She's not an angel, Mam, you snap. Unbidden, thinking of a tiny grave. You told her why it bothered you so much. She still got snippy. No one likes a chastening. And she can't take it, used to dishing out.

You were so glad when you saw two pink lines on the stick. You'd weed on it in the toilets at work, during your lunch break. Once the test was in your bag, you couldn't wait. You sat there for three minutes listening to people come and go. Bowels and bladders evacuated. Hands washed. Doors closed. It felt a whole lot longer than three minutes. You closed your eyes and counted to a hundred Mississippis. And then you looked. And then you looked again.

You did another two before you told him. It felt too big for it to be the truth. He asked if it was his and then apologized and then he started laughing and he hugged you. I'm sorry, he said. I don't know why I asked you that. I know. Of course I know. I mean, I love you.

You looked at him. You said, I love you too. You both were smiling and it hurt your cheeks.

She kicks the leaves and looks at you and crows. It's more than a laugh. It comes right from her belly, the delight. She takes great pleasure in these little things. You like to see her making *such a mess*. The muck and leaves. Or water, paint and sand.

It's *such a mess*, she says. We'll tidy up. We'll tidy before Dad.

And you will rub the table, sweep the floor and lash her in the bath. When he comes home, the evidence all wiped. And she will hug him, smelling fresh of talc. It doesn't always work like that, of course. But that's what he prefers, and what you want. Clean and perfect. You will have to keep each other then.

Pebbles is cute; you get her to tell Dad some more about him. Pebbles is grey and black with bits of white. His eyes are black as well. Just all black circles.

Across the table, something in his face is cold and strange. You ask him about it later and he says, I don't like it. I don't like the thought of her lying to us. Of something weird that lives inside her brain.

He looks at you. You know what he is saying.

You tell him it is not a lie exactly, more a story. He tells you lies are just what stories are. Lies that got dressed up inside a book. Inside a voice. Inside the television. His voice is thin for a man. It doesn't resonate the way your father's did and maybe that is why at first he didn't scare you. Not until you loved him. Only then.

Your father, older than your mam by far. Died when you were twelve. You don't miss him. Picker of a man. He liked to point out everything about you. Everything you were and all you weren't. He wasn't cruel, it's just the way he worked. Probably, he didn't even like himself.

The feeling of inadequacy sticks. It lingers over you. You change her nappy. Time for potty training soon, you think. It's late, you know. You tried it once before and had to call it quits. It's so hard to know when the right time is. And you can't bear the thought of her sticking out, of other children noticing her difference. Laughing at her. The worry makes you sick.

Pebbles says you're broken, Ella says, looking at you up and down.

Pebbles, you tell her, has no idea what he's talking about. Sure, I'm your mammy. Mammies never break.

He says you are. He says there is a line around your wrist that means you're broken. She blinks at you. Her eyes feel like a slap.

You tell her don't be silly.

Pebbles says roll up your sleeves, she chirps. He says that he can prove it. Her language is very advanced. Everyone who chats with her says it to you. She takes a while to warm up, your child. But when she does, she'd charm anyone. She's special.

You wonder when she noticed the white line. It's very thin. You didn't do it properly. You didn't know back then. You know it now, but you don't want to die and so it's useless. If you tried again, you'd get it right. You play with your sleeve. You roll it up and sit down right beside her. Snuggle into me, love, you say. She does. The soft cotton of her little dress. Her purple leggings. You dress her better than you do yourself.

You touch the soft fabric of your polo neck. You sigh. And then you show her. I have a scar, you say. Around my wrist. A mark like this one here is called a scar.

She looks at you.

It doesn't mean I'm broken, you tell her. It doesn't mean anything at all. It's old.

It isn't old like Pebbles, she says to you. Pebbles is an old, old squirrel. He visits me at night. He licks my toes.

29

Her face is hard to read when she says this. You ask her if she likes it. She says no. It tickles. Makes me feel all wiggly like a fright.

He isn't real, you tell her. He isn't real.

He is, she says.

Inside your head you mean, you say to her. You don't know why you say it. Things inside your head are real as well. You know that.

There's a silence. She looks at you. You go to the fridge and get her a little yoghurt in a squeezy packet. She loves those.

Later on, the two of you are painting. She covers up a sheet all red and pink. And something in it chills you. What is it, love? you ask when she's finished. A neutral voice.

It's what he sees in me. Inside my brain. All red and pink and smushy. She smiles at you. She's looking for attention.

You tell her it is lovely, but you dry it on the table, not the fridge.

You show it to him later. She's in bed.

I don't like Pebbles anymore, you say.

He nods.

Later on, you search the internet for imaginary friends. Not that it is a friend. There are lots of stories: vlogs and articles and lengthy histories. You get caught in a loop. When you get into bed, he is asleep. You're noisier than normal, wanting to wake him. Wanting him to help you turn this creature over in your mind until it's smooth. Until it makes sense. He doesn't budge.

You listen to his rhythmic rumble breath. His almost-snore. There is a little spider on the ceiling. You watch as it weaves itself a home, legs rotating. It looks like dance but it's an artless thing.

She doesn't join you in the bed that night. In the morning you give her a sticker. You can feel the circles round your eyes, the black bags filling up with sleep and worry. You are aging.

Your mam comes over and Ella watches cartoons. Little face lit up by the screen. Underwater adventures they are having. She loves the water. Playing with it, swimming. Being submerged. You don't know how much she understands. Some of this science stuff is new to you and she is only three. You make a pot and ask Mam about Pebbles. She says it's normal. Just a normal thing. A lot of children have them.

But the things he says … You trail away. You do not want to tell her. There is no need to dig a dead thing up.

Mam thinks it is her cleverness. That Pebbles can say bad things, the things she can't. She's working out a way to be bold without being bold. You should punish her, she says.

You hate the thought of that. It isn't fair. For something Pebbles did.

Pebbles and Ella are the same thing, says Mam. She made him up. He's her.

That can't be right though.

Ella runs in, laughing, open-faced. The two of you shut up. Discussion over.

When he gets home that evening, you ask him about getting a psychologist.

Or a play therapist. You're emptying the dishwasher, and he is drinking decaf on the armchair.

No, he tells you. He doesn't want to get her into that sort of thing. Not this early.

What do you mean? you ask.

This Pebbles thing. It's obviously getting to you. That's probably why she's doing it. Attention.

His voice.

But then … you say, hands slowing as they wipe the water pooling on the bottom of the cups. The little ponds that make your cupboards pucker if you do not dry them off.

If you start to treat her like she's mentally ill, then she might start to act that way, he says. She's only three. It's just a normal phase. She'll grow out of it.

You do not like the way he looks at you when he says mentally ill.

Ella comes into your room that night. She snuggles into you and he's asleep. You turn your back to him and hold her tightly. She is crying quietly to herself, like grown-ups do. You ask her what's the matter.

He wants to eat my toes, she says. He wants to eat my toes. I need my toes.

You tell her it's okay. And don't be frightened. Mammy's here. No one will eat your toes while Mammy's here. You rub her back and she is soothed and gentled. She believes you. You think about repressed emotions. You think about imaginative play. You think about a shadow-dappled squirrel, curled up like a bird's nest on her peaceful little tummy. Nestling. Making itself at home.

It might be time, you think and he agrees, to look for crèches. Help her socialize. It's never been a problem for her, really. You go to playgroups with other mums you know. To the little park behind SuperValu with the climbing frame and all the swings. It's a nice walk. You can feed the ducks as well, if you've a mind to. There's a sign up. Do not feed the squirrels. They attack. She cannot read but recognizes letters. And you always tell her what things say. Even with graffiti. That says the F-word, love. It isn't nice. Were you wrong to tell her truths like that?

Perhaps the warning lodged inside her brain. Manifesting Pebbles.

He is stronger now. She gives him bits of dinner at the table. One for me and one for Pebbles, she says, eating them both. He's in her now, you see, and not outside her. He's planted in her brain. He's taking root.

I am older than you, she tells you on the potty. I am older and younger than you at the same time. Isn't that funny. She giggles as the urine hits the plastic.

You snap at her. Tell her to shut up. And then you hold her as she cries. It isn't her. It's Pebbles that you hate.

You take her to the GP. He tells you it is normal at her age. Kids are weird, he says. I wouldn't worry. But you do.

She opens up a teddy. Eats the stuffing.

Smears poster paint in circles on the walls. Smooth circles. Almost perfect. Later, when they're safely wiped away, you wonder should you have snapped them on your phone. For evidence. You're building a case study of your own child.

But no one sees how much there is to fear.

In the bath, you see there's poster paint on her torso as well. Whorls and dips surround her little stomach. How did she manage that beneath her clothes?

You rub it off and do not meet her eye. Your hands itch to shake her. Shake her till the *crazy guy* falls out. It doesn't work that way, she says. It doesn't work that way, Mammy. The water's tepid but your fingers boil. You yank her out.

You are spending the night at your mother's. You have taken Ella. He doesn't like to be left with her alone. He loves her, but he has a busy week. At work. Not like you. He needs his space to breathe. Yourself and Mam are talking about Pebbles. She's telling you that it will be okay. Your cousin's little girl had one as well. Blamed it for the bold things that she did. Used it to ask for treats, that sort of thing. She just grew out of it.

Was it a squirrel?

No. It was a badger.

She takes a long slug of tea and you hear yourself refusing to be comforted. There is a danger there she doesn't see. Your voice is shrill and peevish and you hate it.

How's she sleeping? Mam asks.

You say better. Sometimes she still crawls in. We don't mind, really. Be sleeping in her own bed long enough.

And how's himself?

You roll your eyes. The same. Thinks that maybe we should have another. Probably to take my mind off Pebbles.

She dips a yellow biscuit in her tea. It's pocked with little marks. And now it's melting. Her mug fills up with residue of crumb.

It's like, you say. It's like Pebbles is a story. Or a ghost. Or a symptom. And I'm not sure which is worse.

There's no such thing as ghosts, your mother says. She rises from her chair, and goes to the medicine press. Unblisters her sleeping tablet, fills a small glass of water from the tap. The movement of her throat, and a small grunt. The day is over.

But you know better. Tied down on the bed to stop you doing damage to yourself, you'd hear him coming. Smell the body spray and hear the rustle. Crisp and clean the fabric. And you would close your eyes. It wasn't real. If you didn't open up a slit it wasn't true and it would all be over. Hands that traced your body. Only checking. Searching you for symptoms in the night.

In your memory it is invisible. A collection of creaks and smells and half-remembered touches. Sharp and fuzzy all the same at once.

Anything you did in there was crazy. All you had to do was be yourself and they would warp it into something else. Your truths were lies to them. You learned theirs and then they let you out. You're never going back. Even now, an adult and you fear it. These things are a revolving door, they say. We'll see you soon.

You never even drive by there these days.

It wasn't you. You are a different girl.

She doesn't crawl beside you in the night. Your eyes are open, wishing that she would. She is asleep. Your Ella is asleep and she was perfect. She was born perfect and she broke. Something fucked her up and wove a squirrel in her brain and how could you have missed it? How could you have missed the horrid lurk?

You want her to have a safe imagination. The kind that wants to be a fairy princess. The kind that makes her brave instead of scared. A little chink of light through the window casts an obelisk on Mam's floor. He didn't even text to say goodnight. Your feet are softly bare on wood and carpet. Down the stairs and water. Up again.

She is sitting on her bed talking to nothing. You can't make out the words. They are soft and quiet. Her inside voice. She clams up around strangers, all suspicious. Then once she knows you, she can tell you things. You have to earn her friendship. It's probably a decent way to be.

You turn into your room, resisting the urge to interrupt whatever Ella's up to. She'll only want to crawl in with you, and you don't want any comments about big girls sleeping in their own beds in the morning. You've enough on your plate. More than enough. You brush your teeth, cleanse and moisturize, change into your nightdress, and send him a goodnight message with a cute photo of Ella, before you shut your eyes and try to drift.

You must have slept because the screaming wakes you. A primal sound. A rabbit in a trap. A sound you've never heard her make before, not even when she had that ear infection.

It isn't far but oh you run so fast. And your Ella is there in bed all curled in pain. Holding at her feet beneath the blanket. You squeeze her by the shoulders. She's still screaming and she cannot speak. There's blood around her mouth and on her hands. You peel the blanket back. Her little feet. The flesh. You grip your daughter tightly in your arms. And you clamp shut your jaw and close your eyes. Just for a second. You need to remain calm. You need to think.

It will be all right, loveen, you say. We will fix this. It will be all right. The inside of your eyelids isn't working. There's a little red beneath the blackout. Worrying your brain. The screaming stops. She's crying now. She's telling you it hurts. You say I know. You eye the bone through skin and get your phone, some ice. Mam sleeps through everything, and you don't wake her. You don't want her to see what Pebbles did.

Later in the hospital, he sits with her. Her feet in socks of freezer bags, elastic bands that pinch around the top. You couldn't think what to do. It looks stupid. He looks stupid, helpless in his chinos. He holds her in his lap. Stroking her hair, which she has never liked. He wants to be at home. For this not to be happening. And you do too. You are both so tired, and so afraid. You stand at the coffee machine, put your money in and make your choices. You listen to the gurgle in its bowels. When the boiling darkness pours you'll drink it up like medicine. You'll choke it down. You'll swallow it like life.

The Bockety Woman

When my mother's father was a child, he lived in a cottage that became a shed when he finally got the farm. It had grey walls when I was small and the roof was corrugated iron. I never saw it differently to that, so I felt sorry for my little Grandad, growing up in the big dank shed with hay on the floor and plywood in the windows instead of glass.

There were three of them, and their mother and their father in the house.

When I was little, it looked like it had always been a shed, full of bags of things, and dark with spades on the walls and a big thing like pliers for making bullocks out of little bulls. I would go inside and my mother would point out the different rooms, and what they had been. When Grandad was a boy though, things were different. It was a house back then, with fields around and stones and neighbours close but not too close for comfort. That would have suited me. I always liked my space when I was small. I like it now. When people want too much it makes me nervous. To look at you. To touch you. To say things and to hear things and to listen. To eat you up in disappointed bites, like sandwiches at funerals.

According to my mother, my great-grandmother was very beautiful and she always had a scarf and a brooch and she wore lipstick too sometimes as well. Everyone thought she was elegant and my great-grandad was mad about her. Marriages in those days weren't always about love so they were lucky in their little house. And children can be hard. The one of her was not enough to do all of the woman's work accruing. They didn't have hoovers or washing machines back then. They had to sweep the floor and beat the rug out on the washing line and do laundry in the stream and get water from the well for cooking and doing the dishes. That's a lot for anyone to do. So my great-grandad thought about what he could do to make things easier on her.

It's hard for a woman to admit that she needs help, especially an elegant woman. They're supposed to be unruffled, get things done and not bother anyone. Keep the head down and get on with it. Be peaceful and beautiful and streamlined and in motion. Like a swan that glides across the water, not a heifer loping down the road.

My great-grandad was running the farm and the children were steps-of-stairs small so they couldn't really help. He bought her a sewing machine. And that was something. She needed more. And so he bought a person. It makes sense in a way. We package ourselves so people choose us. Squeeze dead-eyed into bras before we've boobs. Looking down, you're scared that they will come but still you want them. All we want is what everybody has. And maybe more.

You could get a person from out of the workhouse then to help you if you wanted. Workhouses were full of poor people, or people with no families to mind them. And it could be a kindness as well to take them in. I don't know how you went about choosing who would help you. Like a job interview or a hiring fair or what. But my great-grandad came back with this bockety little woman who looked like she'd be no help. Her legs didn't work, she'd been born that way, so she kind of snaked around on the floor to get where she needed to go. Her arms were fine. She could do anything with the arms.

I don't know what my great-grandmother thought of the bockety woman, or if she had a hand in bringing her inside their house to mind the things and children. She liked her later on. Pretty women often like women who aren't threats and sure who'd run off with a bockety woman.

Some people who are bockety like to sit down and complain about how bockety they are and that's no good to anyone. She wasn't like that. She didn't talk about the children's 'two good legs' the way their mother sometimes did so pointedly beside her. She was fun. She'd plough down to the stream and wash the clothes, baskets on her back or pulling them with teeth. She must have had good teeth for all her poverty.

I can't imagine how people open bottles, pull at plastic floss. My teeth are soft chalk, crumbling, all give and no resistance.

The children loved the bockety woman and my mother would tell me the story, the way her father had told it to her when she was small. She would tell me how many legs I had and that I'd the use of them and list the jobs to do around the house. The bockety woman had to scrub. Down on hands and knees. Or hands and legs. She was always down on hands and legs. And never up.

She loved the children. She loved their little faces. She can't have been all good. If I were bockety, it would make me cross. Angry at the things my body couldn't do. I get that way already. Looking at the television, all the slender women. Rail thin. Nothing poking over their elastics and

I worry I'm too much and not enough at the same time. And haven't I two good legs? And shouldn't I starve? Shouldn't I starve myself to be as good as them.

Did she never rage? I never asked. Did she never hate my great-grandmother and her husband and her kids and little scarf? Did her mouth fill up with blood from champing down on an angry, lonely tongue?

When my mother tells it, Delia was a saint. That was the bockety woman's name. But women are not saints. Not even saints are. All of us have anger. Burrowed in the marrow of our bones, running up our spines and tensing muscles. Anger pulses through. How do you live through days where nothing seethes?

How do you keep on dragging over the grass, your little gut all wet from dew and panting with the effort of it all? You're strong. They couldn't do what you have done and you only do these things because you have to. What if there were other ways to be? Did she never want to die from how it was? Did nothing hurt her?

People talk a lot about resilience. Offering things up. My mother offers me up like a sacrifice a lot. Looking at my mouth and thinking *eat* and thinking *eat* and when I eat she's analysing bites and I. Am. Trying.

They had nothing back then. Nothing. But they kept on going. Delia kept on going. She had to for the children. I don't know what they paid her. If they paid her. Probably in the roof over her head. In food and bed and water. She had to work. She had to work to stay, she had to please them. Love grew though. With children love can grow so easily. They're soft. The world hasn't carved pores into them and filled them up. Hasn't etched the stretches on their thighs.

Eat, she says. Then, softly: For fuck's sake. She thinks it is a thing I do to her. On purpose. Sometimes she is right.

But not entirely. One bite on the plate of this is spite. A little sprig of greenery. A cherry. It's me and her. The two of us. I'm all she has. All she has is me. And I have so, so many things. There's such a lot of things for me to do. And I am tired.

What happened to the bockety woman, Mam, I ask. To Delia. She looks at me. An apple rests between us. I slice a sliver off. Push it through the maw.

When I was little, I was all for stories. Hated food. Even then I always hated food. One more bite she'd say. And then I'll tell you. I can hear her think it. Up my spine. I hear it up my spine and work my jaw.

They all got sick. My great-grandmother caught it, and so did Delia. And the pretty woman died, and the bockety woman lived. On my great-grandmother's deathbed she had asked Delia to take care of the children. To mind them well. And so that's what she did. She was loyal and hardworking.

Apple taste is soft and artificial in my mouth. Golden Delicious. I like a little sharp beneath my sweet. The mildish pulpy texture feels like rot. We all begin to rot. Food inside your stomach rots as well. It breaks down quick. But you can still outwit it.

My great-grandmother buried in the ground and in the cottage just a man and Delia and the children. It wasn't right but still it wasn't like she could get married. Who would have her? Who would have anyone at all? We're all so human. Delia on the floor, curled up on the hay, a massive hairless cat with apple cheeks. The children there. The children were her reason for it all. And then they grew.

You feed things and they grow. Up and out. Soft fat of the apple meat. The bony little pips I'll shit out later. Apples. Milkless tea. And sometimes toast. One slice.

Crusts off. No butter. I know it's bad but I keep wanting things.

But her. What did she want? What was she after? Sliding through the mud like slug to beer. I cannot stand the broken things around me. They pad and fumble through. They offer things to gods and carry on. I want things offered up to me. I want an altar. For my sacrifice I want an altar. Look at me and love me. Don't come closer. In a church, there's places not to step. You can't go there I'll say. It's mine, it's mine. And they will leave me fruits and eggs and loaves and I will leave them rot and be replaced. I want so hard to matter. My mouth. My two good legs.

The children ripened. They married and they moved. Her work was done. Come live with us, they said. Come be a person. Crawl out of the story of the martyr. No, she said. They didn't ask again. People do not give you second chances when they're used to taking. Hard iron of the handle of the bucket. Splintered wood. Cold water.

The colder you are, the more it burns your skin. The more the padding wears. If you want to lose weight, leave your coat at home, don't bring a jumper. I was walking home and it was cold one day and I was hungry. I sat on the side of the road. I opened up my book. And pulled and plucked and wadded, shoved and ate. A journey's worth of chewing in the paper. All you need's three leaves, rolled and curled and wadded. And you put them in your mouth and chew and chew and chew and feel so guiltless.

And after my great-grandfather came home with this bockety woman, didn't she work very hard for them for years? And when my great-grandmother died, didn't he fall in love with her? And she stood up. Uncurled her twisted back, her little nape, and wiggle-stretched her toes and scratched her ankles. True Love, she said. True Love was what I needed all along. And he said will you dance with me my darling and the children were so thrilled with their new mother that they didn't miss the old one but a little. And she was small and finely built, even at her full height.

And love is what it takes to fix us all.

She died back in the place they got her from. They never saw her after she said no. I brushed the grass-wet off my two good legs and took the long way home for cardio. My heart. My heart. My heart.

Hen

You're reaching for a razor from the shower floor the first time that you spot it, gathered in the plughole, purple-red. You assume it's yours at first or his until you scoop it up and the light catches it. A wave of disgust hits you. You're not a squeamish sort of person, really, and don't think anything of cleaning out the hair that's grown by people in this house, but there is something in this strange intrusion that has you tasting bile. There are times when other people's bodies encroach – flecks of urine on the rim of the toilet seat, a tampon wrapped in toilet tissue lingering in the bin, a finger smudge, a little twist of thread, clung to a button. And you can always trace it back. But this. This hair. It's different and it frightens you. You hate it. You can't exactly pinpoint as to why. You stare at it as though it were a clue, a sort of riddle. Something to decipher, ferret out.

His is brown, and far softer than yours, dull as bark, and slightly wavy. You notice sometimes colours in the sun, little strands of red and black that twine through. His stubble, when he has it, is very red, though salt-and-pepper weaves through it now. He's older. You don't mind that. Think it makes you special. Keeps you young, as middle age approaches. And you were always blonde, once you were old enough to make the choice.

Fifteen years old when you began to dye. A bottle from a pharmacy that only half worked, but you kept on going. And it suited you. You don't remember what you were before. Your childhood hair looks different shades in different photos. Depending on the lighting and the sun. You recall some strands would bleach to ginger. You would pluck those out and keep them in your pocket. You don't know why you did that. Children just do strange things you suppose. And you were very normal, as they go. You've always been a normal sort of girl. He makes you special. He has chosen you. And that is something.

It isn't yours. It isn't anybody's that you know, that henna-purple shade. Who would, at your age? There's more again, you pull at it and pull and it keeps coming, scum-pitted and thick and smooth as braids. You stroke it with your fingertips and feel a shiver moving up your spine, as though this matted glob of strands could bite, or threaten. Of course it's tangled. In the plughole, that's what happens. You comb your own strand from it easily. The golden threaded through. You hold the hair up to your face and look and look.

Cup it in the hollow of your hands, a tufted clump of something like a question. You stick it on the wall for him to see.

This hair came from a head, presumably. It isn't yours. But it is in your shower. Yours and his. The house you bought together, nine months in. They said that it was too quick, your mum and dad. But, at this stage of life, you know your mind. You know the things you want. And you want him. A house can keep a man. A house is hard to leave behind you, lonely. Not that he would. You think about it though. Love isn't tangible. Can't hold it in your hand. Can't eat it up.

Scrolling through the people that you know, you dry yourself and moisturize your skin. You shave your legs every second day; you hate to see the dark bumps coming. He likes your legs and breasts to be all soft. You work so hard at being like somebody's idea of a woman. There are always things to peel from you, to pluck and smooth, eradicate and soften. Your body's worse than the house, you think sometimes, for maintenance. Little cracks appear. You put the bright ring on your hand before you brush your hair. It's been a year, and now it feels like it is part of you, a little piece of body that means love. That means somebody wants you for forever. Visibly. So other people notice.

The guests you've had do not have hair so purple-ginger bright. So teenage girl. A lot of people had that hair back then, you muse, you don't see it so often now. But still, you run your fingers through your own, remember brassy-bright of it the first time. Sure, you didn't know what you were at at all. Before the internet, you read the pamphlet in the little box and followed orders. You needed toner and you know that now. You didn't then. It took you years to find it. You've gone through all the shades: sun-kissed, golden. Platinum was dry and almost white. You worried it would break but still felt beautiful. You throw on the diffuser, set to work with paddle brush and roundy brush and tongs. Your honey highlights filter dark and bright. They're expertly applied. I never skimp on hair is what you tell them. Anyone who compliments your shade.

Henna's how you get that purple-red. Thick as mulch, you lash it on like turf-soup, leave it harden. Friend of yours called Sarah used to do it. Shower caps on, you'd dye together. Hers would come out uglier but softer. You would smile and tell her she looked gorgeous. Eyeing yours and knowing that you'd won.

He doesn't even notice. The clump is still stuck there when you get home, and even there next morning. And more hair in the plug hole to pull out. The selfsame shade. Would whoever it is not have noticed? Would they not have the manners to peel off their unwanted stranger's hair and fecking bin it? You roll the ball much bigger. You've ratted it into a scouring thing. A vivid Brillo pad. You sigh and shrug. It's just a little hair. And it means nothing. Drying on the shower into even brighter shine. It isn't pretty, you tell yourself. It isn't pretty. It is just a lump of something dead. And it means nothing. Fibres that collect are not suspicions. And you don't know how interlinked the water systems are. It could be something oozing in from someone else's pipes. You peel it off and lash it in the bin. It lingers there.

When you were very young, you heard somewhere – you want to say from Grandad but you don't quite remember – that birds use hair from head to build their nests, they weave in fibres through the feathers, twigs, the twiney tails of cows and coarse ones of horses. And you loved birds. You loved them as a child. The soft and singing things, and they could fly. There was something light in them. A thing that you desired. Small and soft and pretty, even then, meant better than the rest. Meant something wanted. And you helped the birds. In sunshine, you would take the pocket-strands and leave them out. You haven't touched that memory in a while. And something in it makes you warm and sad. The child you were. The child had something kind in her. You have it still, you think. You place the toothbrush buzzing in your mouth and move it round until the timer clicks. You brush too hard, the dentist told you once. You're sloughing off your gums, they won't grow back.

Hen

You smooth your makeup gently on your face. Your brush is oily and you need to clean it. Primer first, concealer, eyes, nose, little spots that gather on your chin. Then foundation, blusher, mattifying powder. You look porcelain-flat. A gilded girl. It's not your face at all. It's different colours and it's different shapes. You'll look like this, you think. On your wedding day. But maybe more. You'll make more of an effort for the wedding. Eyelashes on eyelashes. Diamanté accents shining on your nails. You don't get gels done usually. They leave your nails in bits when they come off. You will though, for the wedding.

But the hair.

He's already left for work this morning, while you were asleep. He has a long commute, he works long hours. It isn't like you're used to him around. Not all the time. He loves you. He tells you this. He wants you for his wife. Your face is paler underneath the skin upon your skin. Your pupils shrink. You wonder where the hair began. What sort of head the shaft attached itself to. Follicle after follicle. You can't. Your breath quickens, and you square your shoulders. There isn't someone else. It's you he wants.

You find one strand the next day in the shower. It is long, longer than your hair. Princess length, tumbling softly halfway down a back, tossed elegantly across a shoulder. Blanketing an understanding look. Someone who gets him. You always get up early. She would not. She'd curl up in the pale crook of his shoulder, and he wouldn't brush her off for being warm. A hot-water bottle, he calls you sometimes. And you're not one. You're a cold thing, needing comfort. Needing to be held when he does not.

Here it is again, in the sink at work. Always near the water, you think. Always there. Is it someone from the office? You wonder. Then you tell yourself it's no one. It's only your imagination. Doubt. Doubt is normal when it comes to weddings. Your mother told you when you came home for the engagement party – Champagne and little vol-au-vents on big fat plates that everybody scoffed. It cost them money, but they really love you. And it is the sort of thing that's done. That people do. You like to get it right.

Hours trail away. You're filing paperwork today. Typing, sorting, rearranging things. You have appointments, but it's mostly admin. You look forward to them in a way you do not normally. You have time to prepare today. They punctuate the day like little dots. The blond man smiling at you in his cheap suit. The woman in her fifties with your hair. Shorter, but the colour is the same. You look at her hand. Wedding ring, diamond and eternity ring. They give that to you if you stay the course. A prize for wiving. She's positive about it. Smiling tightly. You assure her things are going to turn. You can't be sure but she has assets. Solid things that you can see and touch. And that is something. Money's just a concept, in the end. Of course you need it. Everybody needs it.

The woman smiles at you. She smells like airport perfume. You spritzed that on yourself when you went to Prague with him. Where he proposed. A lot of people do it in a restaurant. He wanted to be far away with you. Just by ourselves, he said. Just by ourselves in Prague. He loves that city. Wanted you to love it too. You don't. I mean, you do because of the memory. His body kneeling down, his face to yours. But there is something that you get in cities. The *I could live here* feeling. A little bit like love. Like fancying a place. It wasn't there. You didn't feel connection. Pretty though. A gothic sort of pretty. And it rained.

Back at home, you pack the weekend bag while dinner cooks. Scroll through pictures, messages from people.

Hen

Enjoy it hun.
I'm sorry won't be there.
Luv You! Excited.
Get Ready!

You fold your dress. You've packed three different options for the night. You don't know how you'll feel. What you will be. A hen is such a weird name for a woman. Fat and feathered, resting on an egg with pinhole eyes. You stash your smaller makeup bag, essentials, little extras, toiletries, and tights and spare tights and shoes. The kind of underwear that's meant to hurt you. Suck your stomach in and hold your legs. The bands around your thighs make tiny sausage links. You're thin already. He likes that about you. But you have a tummy sticking out, and you don't like to see it in your dresses. As small as possible. As little of you there, so that people look and notice nothing flawed. There could be a gym there. Not that you will go. But if you wanted. You pack leggings, t-shirt, runners, bra. Just in case. In case you get the chance. You sit upon your bag to make it close. There's too much in it. Too many possibilities for where the night will go.

He isn't home till late. You eat together. You tell him you're excited for the hen, and he smiles. His teeth shine like the hair did in the bleaching bathroom light. He's handsome. You touch his cheek. He asks you what was that for. You tell him that you love him and he smiles. And it is true. You do. You're sure you love him. But now there is a sort of question mark. A slender crack. And you can feel it growing with each hair. It's only hair. You shrug it off. Hair is not the proof of anything. It's not a lipstick stain, a naughty text.

You fall asleep on your side of the bed. His breath is deeper, faster in the night. You put your cold hand on him and he flinches in his sleep and rolls away. You run your hands along the sheet beneath you. Searching for a purple-scarlet sign. It's much too dark of course for such endeavours. You hold his scent inside you like a prayer.

The morning filters through the curtain chink, and your alarm beeps. He groans and turns. You get it on the first beep. You always rise about an hour before him. So much more getting ready. In the shower, there's nothing in the gutter. You shove your fingers as far in as they'll go. It's empty. And maybe that's the end of it, you think. Any house can have a little ghost. When you were small, the doors would bang of their own accord. Your parents always told you it was Johnny. Johnny the ghost who liked to close the doors. It was the wind. But sometimes weird things happen. And just because you do not have an explanation yet, doesn't mean there isn't one. There's something that you'll find out soon that will burn your worries up. Turn them into ash-and-crumble nothings. They're only burning till they're all used up.

Work flies. It's a busy day and everybody wants a piece of you, some insights on a project. Some advice. You're competent and sometimes you're the only one that is. They lean on you. They're asking you for something all the time. And it can be exhausting. But it's nice. It's nice to have a talent. To be good at things that need doing.

After work, you drop your car off to the house. It's quiet. The lights are off. If you were a burglar, what would you think? Or if you were a stranger. Does the sitting room look happy through the glass? You tried your best with it, nice art up on the wall. A statement armchair. You don't know what it says about you though. You turn your key inside the door, key in the code for the alarm, grab your bags and wait. You'd love a cup of tea, but Jean will be on time. She always is.

Jean's car is bigger than yours. She picks you up. She gives you a feather boa and you giggle. You tell her that you hope that's all there is. You don't want any of that willy stuff. She crooks an eyebrow. She has something planned for you, you know.

Jean is your chief bridesmaid. You've known her since school. And then in college. She did sports science, but you shared a flat. You were there the night she met her husband. And you did this for her two years ago. It was a lovely wedding. You wore purple feathers in your hair. Same colour as your shoes. A bright green dress. And everybody said that you looked stylish. Put things together in a certain way and people will believe that about you. You saw it in a magazine. Hunted it down. And that's not style. That's copying. Or armour. You hadn't met him then. All by yourself at weddings is a struggle. I mean, there's no one there to hold your hand. To nudge you when you well up at the vows. No hand, flat on the small of your back. Steering you through rooms and into chairs. You're your own guide. You forage for yourself. And you don't miss it. The things that people say can feel like knives.

You met him through a friend. You hadn't done the app thing yet. You'd built a profile, then deleted it. You know it's normal now, but you couldn't bring yourself to want out loud. There's a whiff of something desperate in you. Something you try to hide. You see it sometimes, there in other people. You recognize it, and you feel contempt.

He didn't say goodbye to you this morning. Jean hums along. The road to Amy's house. You think of his hard bulk in the soft bed, sucking in the final bits of sleep. And he won't see you for two days and nights now. It's not a lot. But just to say goodbye. You ventured in and kissed him and he grunted. That was how he left it. Love of your life. It isn't like a book. But these things never are. And when he kisses you, his tongue is meat and so is yours. It's just two muscles touching. You feel it trickle down between your legs. But still. It isn't magic. Just biology. He's not a prince. He's just another man. But he has chosen you and so you love him. Love that about him. That you're the thing he wants. He had a little speech prepared. A ring you'd pointed out in a shop window. It didn't fit. You had to make it bigger, but on that day you forced it on and smiled. You were wearing it. You didn't care. And you were getting married. And you love him.

Amy and Jean are telling you they're taking you to Laois, to Leitrim, Carlow, Wicklow, Cork. They're giving you no clues. They've brought a blindfold. If you ask questions, they will make you wear it. You're laughing at their threats and eating a Mars bar. Jean bought a whole plastic bag of treats. Feck the diet, she says. As though she needs to diet. As though she can't eat everything she wants and still stay trim. Jean is a fitness instructor. She's thirty-four, but still looks like a child. Her and Anthony are trying now. They're trying. And soon a little thing will take root in her belly. It will grow and they will have a child and you will not. Your friends are always doing things ahead. And it is fine. I mean, you're happy for them. Your hand clutches your stomach. I'm as fat, you say, and she throws her laugh at you and says you're lovely. She has to say it though. You are her friend.

There are rules about things. You have to be delighted when there's good news. You have to be excited on your hen. The car pulls up to a large grey hotel. Jean's face is gleaming. She hasn't makeup on. Sometimes her skin gets oily. She'll look different tonight. You're always done. You show them faces you want them to see. Together. Calm and happy. You are happy. You brush a stray hair off Jean's floral top. That's the kind of friendship that you have. Where it's okay for you to groom each other. She turns and tells you thank you. And she means it. You put the hair in the pocket of your tight high-waisted trousers. You want to hold it up to window light. The feel of it is strange. You don't know why. Something inside you knows it will be red.

You have lunch together in a big gang. Twenty women. Four of them his sisters. Five of them from work, two from your old job. All the girls from college. Some from school. They look at you and smile like you're a puppy. You hug them in a circle one by one. You order just the salad, but the smell of Amy's chips is so amazing that you ask for one and then another one. She spills a little pile onto your plate. The bite out of her mouth. You chew them down.

Before he met you there was someone else. Someone he could have married. Her name was Teresa. And he'd been with her for fifteen years, since they were very small. She moved away. Moved to the States for work. He couldn't go. He had to mind his mother. And by the time she died, Teresa had met another man. A Yank. He never told you this. You gleaned it from his sisters. They have brown hair, like his, but all with highlights. Women have to try to make the most of themselves. Men just cope with having what they have. You don't mean to be sexist. But in general. He cuts his toenails, and he thinks he's great. I mean, he probably is. You've been with men before who looked like wolves once they took off their socks. All the parts that people see all groomed and then a puff of body hair, a growth of nail, a stipple of bright scabs along their legs. What nature gave, she didn't give to everyone. But there's no reason not to try a bit.

You googled her. You tried to get a look. The photos are gone. He doesn't have them up. I mean, he wouldn't. You never search his phone, his laptop folders. It isn't right to poke in someone's life. They have to share it. Still, she niggles at you. She doesn't even have a profile picture. It's just a landscape, sunrise over hills. The view from where she lives now, maybe. From where she works, so far away from him. It takes long fingers to reach across an ocean. Ropes and ropes of tangle-twisting hair.

You take the little strand out from your pocket. You look at it. It's red. It's red. It's red. Your salad's in your mouth and you are smiling. Autopilot. Everybody laughs. And there are goody bags, with sweets and bottles of water. Little cards they've made about the weekend. Amy has done up laminated timetables. Amy would. You smile at her. You tell her: such a teacher. You tell her that they're great. You tell her thanks. You sip your water and you eat your salad. It doesn't fill you but there'll be dinner later. You can wait.

You have a clean white dress. It clings to every curve. The neckline straight across. It's quite severe, but it looks good with your skin and eyes and hair. Like you have a tan. You are the bride. You like reminding people that you're the bride. Not with your words, but with your dress, your posture. This weekend, you're the special one. You're her. You might not ever get the chance again to be the shining thing inside a room. To be applauded. Next time is the wedding. But you're sharing that with him. It's both of you and to you he's the star. He'll look amazing in his suit. And you'll be there. You'll say the words to him and you'll be married. He'll be yours forever. He wants kids. At this time in my life, he told you early, I want to settle down. To raise a family. Grow roots.

Roots that hold you down. He wants the weight of that. He wants commitment. And you're a heavy thing with all your hopes. Jean and Amy sharing the room with you. They cluck and trill about your pretty face, your hair, your dress. You go into the loo to wash your hands and there it is again. A purple-reddish strand. You hold it up. You twist it round your finger. Round and round until it puffs with blood. A little tourniquet above the ring. And did she have red hair. And did he like it?

You wash your hands. You go out to play party games before the dinner. They made him do a video for you, where they ask questions. He scored quite highly on the little quiz. When it's your turn, you answer all but one right. You thought his favourite place would be Prague. But it is somewhere else. A place you've heard of, but you've never been. He didn't suggest it for the honeymoon. He's thinking of the Maldives, or Japan. And was he there with her? You scan his sisters' faces. They are smiling, but it's hard to read. You notice another hair, trapped in the carpet fibres beneath your heel. You peel it off and put it in the bin, and Jean scolds you. You're not at home to tidy up, she says. You don't have to do any of that craic now. Let's make a mess for someone else to clean. You smile at her. You pop a Skittle into your worried mouth. You drink Prosecco.

There are photos of you on the walls. And some of him. They're cute to look at. One of them is from his Debs. It's too narrow to be full. And on his shoulder, you imagine someone's head is draped. A trail of hair. It isn't visible but you can see it. You can see it snuggled warmly in.

He doesn't like that now you think. He doesn't. You alter your expression as you look. You're conscious to project the nicest things. Being touched. And smiles. And being happy. Those are things you are allowed to feel. This weekend's only about parts of you. The happy parts. The other parts for later. For when you're by yourself. You like to clean. The house. You like to scrub.

He tells you sometimes you should hire a cleaner. But you just like to do it all yourself. To be the girl who can. To be that woman. Tidy. Pretty. Capable. All the wifely qualities he needs. He does like spending time with you. You go for dinners, and you always chat. You never run out of things to say to him. And he does listen. God, you know he does.

You're judging dresses made of tissue paper. You're counting who can fit the most marshmallows in their mouth and making blow-job jokes and screaming laughing. You're thinking of the small crown of a head, coated purple-red. And shedding, shedding. Hair all over. Nudging at your life. They say the right things to you. You say the right things back. Call and response. They're happy for you, you know. And you're lucky.

The dinner's lovely. You have the skinless chicken, two potatoes. Allow yourself dessert. You love a slice of cheesecake now and then. It's like two sins at once. The cheese. The cake. There's wine and more Prosecco with the dinner. And Jean toasts you. She says some lovely things and you well up, say thank you. Shake your head. And all the while, your fingers want to rat around on the floor, under the little cushions on the chairs. They want to search for what you are expecting. It will show up. Something always does when things need ruining. You play with the little tendrils that soften your updo. You pull at one with finger and with thumb, you snag it out. The pain's a bit surprising. It's been a soft, soft day for all your thoughts.

Amy, wide smile pink around the lips, lashes a vodka and Diet Coke in front of you as though it's medicine. Are you all right? she asks you. Are you having fun? You nod your head. It's class girls, thank you, thank you. I can't believe ye went to all the effort. Did so much. Jean kisses your cheek. You're worth it love, she tells you. He's such a lucky man. He really is. Her eyes are glazed with drink. She isn't pregnant yet you think. You love her. You love your friend Jean. She is the best. And when you rang her, to tell her that he'd asked, she was so happy for you. So relieved. You could see her slipping back towards how much you had in common. Recalibrating you inside her head. Friendship's like a marriage. It isn't simple. And it takes some work. She's wearing an electric blue top, and it's silk. A cashmere cardigan. Jean likes good fabric. You pull at the hem of your dress.

Leonie, Laura, Jasmine in a circle with the ladies from the office. Dancing around. Faces open wide. The lights are shining on them. There is a cover band there, playing songs. The lead singer in baggy, torn jeans, holding the microphone like it's a friend. He smiles and twists his eyebrows at the crowd between the songs. The bassist has red hair. A different red, you think. A different red. You rise, all wobbly like a colt. It isn't that you're drunk. You've put away enough. But you feel sober. It's the heels and it's the getting up and thinking dark thoughts when you should be bright. You join the girls and dance. You move your body.

The first boy that you kissed had bleached hair, braces. You met him at an underage dance thing. Everyone was drinking. You had half a naggin in your purse. And he was wearing the t-shirt of a band you played over and over again while getting ready at home by yourself. It felt like fate. And maybe it was. He listened to you talk and then he kissed you. He didn't take your number when he stopped.

When you and Jean lived together, before she met Anthony, you would go out dancing, and you'd prowl. Less obviously than men do, dancing up to friends, and moving on to whoever will have them as the night progresses, grabbing out at arses, breasts and backs. At flesh. At bits of flesh beneath your clothing. Sometimes all you felt like, all you were. And you would eye a person. You would pick them. And you'd move your body, tilt towards them. You wouldn't smile. But you'd make eye contact if it were there to make. You'd drink the drinks they bought you. Toss them back and grin at them and plan. A woman is a different sort of creature to a man. Another vampire. Everyone has needs. To be consumed. Or held. Or something. Something.

You still move your eyes across the room, even now. You pick him out. The person that you'd want. If you hadn't finished with your wanting. If you hadn't started with your life. The world's too big sometimes. Everyone's another possibility. A road that you could walk. So many futures. Sometimes you think that all the parts of growing up, the milestones, just make the world smaller, smaller still. A little life. An easy little life. A normal man. A love story. A family. The biggest day. You want the biggest day.

You look amazing, Laura yells at you. The music is too loud to hear the words. You're reading lips. You flap your hands at her, the sign for thank you. Thank you but you're wrong. You're having fun. An arm wraps around you. Stocky man who smells of something stale. He's in a flannel shirt. He looks like him. You hadn't picked him out. You push his chest away, and say I'm taken, flashing him your ring like it's a power. He tells you that you aren't married yet, but his eyes are already scoping out the next choice and the next one. All the pretty things you've gathered close.

Leonie's getting sloppy, and she grins at him. You think you'll have to watch her. She's always far too friendly with the men. Her heart is always breaking. It's part of what you love about her. There's always something interesting to talk about. A problem to dissect. Your hands run through your hair. You snag a tangle. Examine it, and let it drift to the ground. In the dim red light, it is the wild red colour of your bird's-nest childhood strands. Blonde reflects a multitude. You could be her, you think. You could be the one. But so could she. Or she. And it was time to make his world small, to settle down. He met you at that point. And you are glad. You're glad of him. You're glad. And you deserve him. You're a lovely woman. You'll wear white. You'll have a little basket full of flip-flops just beside the dance floor. Jean had one at her wedding, that was nice. You like the little touches.

The first time that you slept with him, you went into the bathroom afterwards. To have a wee, in case you'd get a UTI. When you came back, he was fast asleep. He trusts me, you thought. It wasn't that at all. He's just the kind of man who's used to feeling safe in different places. You like that in him. Rubbing off on you. He's going off to Westport with the lads next weekend. Paintballing. He's been before. You traced the small round bruises on his skin. Your heart was tender. Something about taking care of things. You want a baby. But you can't be sure. I mean, there are so many things that can go wrong. Inside a person and outside a person. Jean tugs your arm. She has a tray of shots. You knock one back.

You're in the bathroom putting on your lipstick. Brushing hair. There is a girl who's sitting in the corner. She has a box of things. Tampons, perfumes, little hair elastics. Lollipops. You're never sure exactly what to give. You lash a euro in her patterned saucer. She smiles at you and thanks you. Her face is almost orange, there's a line. She's thinner than you, wearing a tight black polo-shirt with the logo of the bar on it. You see a strand of something in the sink. You look at her; she's rearranging little piles of tissues. You pull it out. You have to pull it out.

His sister Fiona bumps in through the door. She's texting with her clutch purse in the crook of her elbow. It looks awkward. You tell her hello. You have the sad wet strand of hair clinging to your palm and down your wrist. She looks at you. And you look back at her and pull it off, replace it in the sink and make a face. She asks you if you're having a good night love. You smile at her and nod. She moves her lips. You do not hear the words. She's in the cubicle. You place the palms of your hands flat against the cold hard of the sink. And then you breathe. Collect all of the parts of you that matter. List the good. The way he makes you feel. His face. His face.

A girl emerges from a toilet cubicle. She takes eyeliner from her little purse, applies it to the underside of her eyelashes so carefully. Pulling out the skin. It's almost medical. Her hair is henna-red. You know you're staring. She knows it too. She looks at you, clocks your little sash and the tiara. Smiles congratulations on her way out the door. You blink at her. Your lips try to shape thank you. You've been here for too long. You need to move.

You find Jean. Jean, you say. And look at her. She puts her hand on the small of your back. The way he does. You love it when he does that. You love his hands on you. And even if. Jean, you say to Jean, it isn't me. I think I could be anyone.

Her features rearrange. She shakes her head, and gets you in a cab. The warmth of the seat clings almost painfully to skin. There is a hole in your tights. You don't know when it grew but now it's there. A little fibre poking out the bottom of the ladder. Your fingers grasp at it. And pull and pull. She's telling you about her period. About it coming, feeling like a curse. Like somebody is laughing at her body. And I can do so many things, she says. I can't do this. I can't do this. You tell her that it's fine. It will be fine. You wind the strand of nylon round your hand. You're ripping them to shreds. You keep on going. You can't discern the colour. But you know. Jean curls her little body into yours. You've left the others at the club. But that's okay. That's okay. You're the bride, clinging to the warmth that builds below her. A soft important thing that someone wants.

Later in the bed, hands worry at the chicken skin on legs. Up and down in ribbons on your body. Deep enough to ease but not to hurt. The soft breaths of the other hens around you. Their hums and twists. They do not sound like him, these pleasant noises. You close your eyes and think of the first dance. Of lacy veil removed. Of jewelled belt. The small fat rose embroidered on your headband. Of being led. Of being beautiful, and feeling safe. You love him and you want him and you're lucky. Purple-red hair on a map. Something borrowed, woven through your nest.

You roost.

You know.

Pearleen

Kate wouldn't have found the lump if her breast hadn't started to hurt. The pain was something to investigate, and when she did hesitantly touch and prod herself, it just got more intense. It was not the normal, swollen sort of pain, more like the feeling of having a really big and painful spot developing, inside of her. Incubating. The lump itself was round and hard to the touch, and moved worryingly around the inside of her breast whenever she poked it, leaving small and painful burrows in its wake. She was aware of it constantly, an insistent hum throughout the day, getting so strong sometimes that she had to make her way to the bathroom and cup her breast and push it in really tight against her chest, like it was a carry-on suitcase that she needed to shut. She bore it for as long as she could, because she found doctors touching her harder to take since what had happened the year before last. And maybe somehow it would go away. Sometimes things did. At fifteen, she had gotten her period twice a month for six whole months, to the point where her PE teacher called her a liar and her mother had to get involved. The GP said to wait it out, that she was still developing. It took a while for things to settle sometimes. She remembered his face, how clean-shaven he was, and the suit he had been wearing. He had a photograph of a woman on his desk, and Kate had wondered if she was his wife.

She was developed now, but still Kate waited longer than she should to ring the doctor and make an appointment, after which she sat on the sofa and tried not to think about it. Listing jobs she had to do instead, the pieces of the house that didn't work. But her hand kept searching for it, remembering. The lump was in her slightly bigger breast, the one nearest the heart.

'The left ones always get a little bigger,' her mother had told her once when she felt freakish. 'Because of the blood supply. People rarely notice.'

Kate's mother was not exactly a font of knowledge and support, but even so, it helped. Kate hadn't thought to confirm that information, never looked it up or asked a friend. It seemed plausible and also made her feel a little better. She didn't need any more than that. But now there was a lump and the quarter-cup-sized difference suddenly seemed menacing, like the extra flesh was some sort of omen, a throbbing sign of horrid things to come.

The doctor felt her up and told her there was nothing to worry about. It moved around, was regularly shaped. Probably fine. They'd get an ultrasound though, just in case. *In case of cancer* went unsaid. Eight weeks she waited, going to work, going to the gym, doing things with friends. Telling no one but her mum for some reason she couldn't fathom. It didn't come up organically, when they talked about their bodies; the fear came from how they'd be perceived by people's eyes. Kate wouldn't know what to say, if someone told her they had sore breasts, except 'that sounds hard' or 'what are you going to do about it' and neither of those things would really help. Sometimes there is no right thing to say. Only degrees of wrong thing. Kate remembered.

There was something about the lump the ultrasound technician didn't like.

'I don't like the look of it,' she said. Her eyebrows were drawn on, but they still expressed concern more than adequately. Kate lay there with her breast covered in gel and her eyes away from the screen, watching the woman scribbling on the chart. It is not nice to be told that someone doesn't like the look of something growing in your body. To feel that there are secrets it will tell a stranger but not you. The brows went down. 'We'll have to get that out.'

And then more waiting.

Kate was in a gown made of paper. She was scared of the anaesthetic because she had read an article online about people who it didn't work properly on. They seem to pass out, but really they are only paralysed, and they can feel everything and hear everything but they cannot move and nobody can tell. And you can't know how it's going to impact you until it's too late. Just stuck there, feeling everything – a nightmare. Still, it felt rude to question the anaesthetist, sure everyone knew how busy doctors were. On the trolley, though. They put a mask on her face and she breathed in and counted down.

When Kate was a little girl, she had gone on holiday to the seaside. Her mum was from the seaside, but she moved inland after she met Kate's dad and they got married. The towels they lay on were grainy from the sand, but warm and soft. They didn't wash them every day, but always hung them up to dry them out. Kate used to press her face into the towels and breathe in and out the sand and saltwater. Sometimes her dad would hold her head under the water till she stopped struggling. Ducking, it was called. They used to do that to witches back in the day.

'Your mother is a witch,' her dad would say. 'Are you one too? Are you my little witch?' And he would duck her. And she would feel scared but also safe, because he'd never hurt her, not her dad. He was tall and had hairs on his belly and in his ears and nose. His swimming togs were blue with one red stripe. Under the water, everything was still. She must have been near drowning once or twice – of course she must – but she remembers feeling really safe there. The rush of water and her own strong heartbeat. Kate never noticed that she couldn't breathe.

Out of the room, into another. Kate was staying over-night. Last time she stayed here her baby died and they had to take it out. It was a different ward in the same place. It smelled the same but the sounds had been a little dif-ferent. Twenty-seven weeks was when her baby died. She moved, she had a heartbeat, then she didn't. She waited two more weeks to be induced. She was supposed to go into labour spontaneously during that time, because her baby was dead and her body should have known that, kicked it out. It chose to clutch the baby close instead. For hours she was pushing, getting poked and prodded and told what to do until finally they opened up her womb and took it out of her that way instead. Kate didn't care at that stage. She felt numb.

When she went back to work, when people called round asking how she was, she heard and dealt and answered through a veil: porous enough to let her move and breathe, but the exterior was quite impermeable. You could not touch Kate now anymore, and even if you did it wasn't really Kate that you were touching. After the baby, people brought her Lucozade and magazines and hand cream. After the baby, people said things to her and moved their heads and touched her with their hands. They knew things about her that she didn't want them knowing. She could see her baby in their eyes. Even now sometimes. A flash of ghost. It had felt a bit like being haunted, being pregnant. Unexpected thumps, and moments when she would be reminded that there was a little person living inside of her. For a while afterwards, sometimes it would feel like she was still inside, and Kate would tap her stomach, or say something to the baby before she remembered that she was alone.

Kate was thirsty so she drank some water. She closed her eyes and opened them again. The curtain was pulled around her bed, but light filtered in through the thin green fabric and the gaps on top. If she squinted her eyes, it was almost like being in a pretend forest.

The surgeon, who she'd never met before – her consultant was on holidays or something, away was all they'd said – looked like he was dressed up as a surgeon for Halloween. He had broad shoulders and a stocky build. Stubble peppered his face, not just his cheeks but all the way up to almost his temples. His incisors were a little bit too short for all his other teeth and it gave his face a bizarre mix of innocence and malice. His voice was surprisingly gentle; she had expected a rumbly kind of gurgle.

'The procedure was successful. However, there was something ...' He didn't seem to quite know how to finish.

'Something?' she echoed, feeling her heart press out and zoom in. When doctors paused, it gave her a specific sort of feeling.

'Yes.' He nodded, his Adam's apple bobbing up and down. She wondered if it would feel as hard and round as her lump had beneath her fingers. Her breast still hurt, but now it was a different sort of pain. He was saying something about calcification. And tiny irritants. 'Most unusual …'

Kate scratched the underside of her bandaged breast. Sweat was pooling there and she couldn't understand what he meant. Individually, the words were comprehensible, but interspersed with staccato *ums* and *ehs*. A distinct lack of fluency, of flow. All in little bits, shattered. Kate couldn't begin to assemble them.

'… sac …'

'What, like a sack of barley?' It occurred to her that she should have said flour. Barley did not come in sacks at all. *It's the Stack of Barley isn't it, the dance?*

He was still talking, fiddling with something in his pocket. He didn't mean a sack as in a sack. A sac of cells, he meant. A sac of special cells. The distinction escaped Kate so he trailed off with a low 'We thought you might want it …'

'Want what? The lump?'

'It isn't just a lump …' And from his pocket, he produced a large, white, iridescent thing. A sort of pearl. Kate took it. It was warm from his hand. She hoped he wasn't sweaty. Sweat damages pearls. They must be carefully kept and carefully cleaned. Kate's granny had given her a pair of pearl earrings just before she died. She rarely wore them. Pearls are so fragile. She would hate to hurt them, melt them with perfume or with dry air. This pearl, this thing, was weighty – it fit exactly into the palm of her hand, obscuring the life line, the love line, and all the other lines she couldn't name. The surgeon was still there. 'And there are more.'

'What?'

'Six or maybe seven. Just growing. We didn't like to … disturb them.'

'Oh.'

'We didn't know. We didn't think we should. Do. Anything. Until we had your consent. Because … because they're lovely.'

He smiled a big unguarded smile for a second, and then his face reset. Kate blinked. The shaft of light where the curtains did not meet was very bright indeed, all of a sudden. She told him she would like some time to think. He made a note, and left. Do oysters ever want someone to take that bit of grit out, Kate wondered. And does it matter, really, what they think?

When the baby came, Kate got to hold her. The baby had a tooth. A little one, to the left of the bottom row. So small and white. A pearleen, Kate called it. There was hair as well, wispy but surprisingly thick. And soft. Her baby's hair was soft. She looked a little like her father and a lot like all the other babies Kate had seen. Only paler. Her fingernails had a sort of cloudy sheen, as if it were wearing subtle, job-interview nail polish. Kate had been waiting to find out the gender. Her baby was a girl. A little she.

Kate's fist around the pearl tightened. Little glimmers of it through her fingers. It was enormous for a pearl. Her breast itched and she thought about the treasure trove within. Six or maybe seven little lumps.

Angel was written on the grave.

'You couldn't call her that,' Kate's mother had said, a bit dismissively. 'She'd have an awful time of it at school.'

'Well, luckily for her, she won't be going,' Kate had snapped, and that had shut her up. Her mother was right though. Kate would have called her something else, if she had been a living roaring thing.

To get a pearl from an oyster, they used to send divers down. There was a story in a book Kate had read about the work they did, the price they paid. Kate supposed it might be kinder now, more ethical, but she couldn't be certain. Things didn't always go the way you'd hope. On the forums, people talked about their rainbow babies. The internet still tried to sell her slings.

The pearl left resting on the pillow, Kate prodded at her milkless breast. She hadn't lactated before or after the baby was born. Her breasts had gotten bigger, stayed bigger, but not a single drop of milk had leaked out. She felt a cluster of small nubbins, bunched together. Puppies in a pile, asleep and growing. Wasn't that unusual for pearls? Part of what made them special was their cloistered uniqueness, softly growing on the tongues of oysters. Well, not exactly tongues. Could oysters think? Not in words, anyway. Maybe just needs and feelings. Kate placed the pearl on the bedside locker, with a nightie tucked around it so it wouldn't roll. It was roughly the size of a ping-pong ball. There was a softness to the way it caught the light. It nestled in the folds of artificial silk like an egg. Kate pushed her hand against her breast and felt for something underneath the skin and through the pain. A precious nest of some sort. A clutch of them to follow, to be hatched.

Black Spot

You pass it always on your way to work, with all the flowers. Petrol station bouquets in cellophane. Carnations, baby's breath and hot pink daisies. Sometimes there are roses from a garden. Or the wilder sort. Marigolds and buttercups and clover. Little bunches picked and wrapped in kitchen paper, cling film or tinfoil. Made at home.

Bunches added, never cleared away. Piles of them are rotting. Petals gone and stalks have melted into rain with time. It makes you sad. It makes you sad to see the care and lack of care at once, all sellotaped together.

In your little Mazda with the heater blasting window mist at full tilt. It ruins your skin. You moisturize but dryness still collects around the nose and when you scratch it's red, not raw, but sore. You look like you've been crying when you get to work a fair amount. In the face but never in the eyes.

You live far out the country, in a house you could afford. You drive when it is dark and arrive when it is getting bright. You leave work when it's dark and get home darker. You stay late most of the time. You have to. People never pick their children up on time and then there's tidying and sorting art supplies and things. Construction paper. Glue. You don't use glitter now. It is forbidden, it gets everywhere. Leanne, the manager, found some in her knickers two Mother's Days ago and said no more.

Leanne is the sort of person who is very comfortable with putting her foot down. Younger than you are. She hasn't worked in the crèche for half as long, but when Michelle retired, she took the reins. You wonder if you'd spoken up, could you have? What you could have done to be that woman. The one who makes things happen for herself.

When Leanne tells you to do things, you resent it sometimes and she feels it. You used to get on better. It's not that you don't listen. It's that she's younger. It's that she doesn't always do her best. She expects you to do the grunt work and you don't get paid enough to like that.

Every morning, every evening. Driving past the flowers. You look at them. You always think *One day I'll stop the car, get out and tidy.* It would be a nice thing to do, but there are reasons not to get involved. You don't know who died here. You don't know who left flowers and for whom. You want a cup of tea. It's getting late.

Maybe in the summer, when it's nice again. Then maybe you could do it. It has been years and still the flowers rot and you do nothing. 42 deaths changed to 43. Then 47. Accident Black Spot.

It's cold today. The storage heater on the wall at work makes little difference. The walls are thin. When the children are indoors it's more bearable. Their bodies little stoves, wolfing down Ready Brek. Spaghetti hoops.

Sometimes their mothers drop them off at half seven, collect them after six. You give them breakfast, lunch and dinner, tea. You hug them when they cry. You're not supposed to now, with child protection, but you always do. Their shrivelled little faces full of woe. You have to give them love. They're hurting, hurting and you're not their mum but you are close enough and you are there.

You look after the preschoolers. Leanne has the after-school club; she helps out different places and does paperwork till half past one. Laura has the babies, small and squat. The wee triangley things. You all help each other out, and there's Paula who is being trained and floats. Leanne was like Paula once. You trained her up. She's good at what she does but so are you.

She wants to buy a house.

Don't bother, you tell her. Time enough when you're a little older.

She doesn't roll her eyes but you can feel her wanting to. You wipe the desks down savagely, scratching them with nails through J-cloth fabric. Every little piece of crayon gone when you are done. Every daub of Pritt Stick.

It isn't enough. Work, home. It isn't enough and still it's all you have and you are tired. You do your makeup in the car on the way there. Cleanse your face each evening before bed with heavy hands. Scrubbing at the corners of your eyes. You do not wear an awful lot of makeup. Just enough to show you've made an effort. Taking pride.

It is November when it happens first. The morning dark and soft, the man on the radio joking about something and his voice is kind. You think he must be handsome in real life. Your hands on the steering wheel are tight. The skin on them is chapping. You should wear gloves. You should put on your gloves.

You're not sure when the beeping starts. You notice it before the little shop where you buy milk when you run out of milk. The light. The seat belt light. But yours is on, you fasten it each morning. Working with the children makes you safe. You wait for the green man, look right, look left. Rub in the soap and put your hands under the water rubbing for a count of ten, a count of ten again. Your hands are clean, and you don't get knocked down. You set examples. The seat belt light is beeping.

It is strange. The car passes three miles down the road, beside a little dormer bungalow with plywood in the windows and no door. You forget about it till tomorrow and the next day and the next.

It always happens on the way to work. The little seat belt light, all red and soft. It doesn't glare. It's like a little sunset. You go to the mechanic on day six. It starts and stops, you tell him. It's always different places.

He shrugs and charges you for being shrugged at. He did lift up the bonnet after all.

Work is softer for the next few weeks. The children come and go. You only hug them loosely round the shoulders. Wipe their noses, tears. Clean them up when they have little accidents. Sometimes they don't make it there in time. And that's okay. You have a box of gender-neutral clothes that you put on them. Things you've bought and things the older children have left behind. The dear departed. You miss them all a little. Wonder how they're doing.

The first ones that you had are almost grown now. You see them in the papers. One or two. Clare who got all H1s in the Leaving. Norman who assaulted someone once. Poor Norman. You remember his sense of injustice. *She stoled my crayon*, shrill across the room. You cut the pieces out and take them home and keep them. Your nieces and your nephews in Australia are in that shoebox too. Your brother's wife remembers you at Christmas. And once a year they clamber in your house, live up on you for weeks and leave you lonely and relieved at once. You love them but you also need your space.

When Mother was alive, you worried they would stop when she passed on. But then she had two heart attacks and died. A big one first, a little one that killed her. And she was in the ground. And that was that.

The beeping keeps on going until you've almost parked for work one day. It punctuates the sunrise. You thought at first that it was something stuck. But still it comes and goes. You start to count the beeps on the days they happen. Twelve. Fifteen. And nineteen. Thirty-six. Different places, houses, shops and flats. And sometimes fields. Just sometimes outside fields. The flowers still collect. The little tributes there, still piling up. Hydrangeas. Blue. Pink. Purple. The same plant but grown in different earths: acidic, basic. You can put lime down to pink them if you want. You like the blue. You think you like the blue.

Madonna hates hydrangeas. You pick up nuggets, driving in the car. Little gossips. Stupid bits of news. You only sometimes read the papers. Sunday's one will do you for the week. There's online, but your connection's slow. When Lucy sends you pictures of the children they appear in rectangles from the top down, unpuzzling bit by bit.

You like real photos. Something you can hold. Can take to work and show them. You think sometimes they don't think you do things. Don't have a life. You do. You go for drinks, meet friends. Go to the cinema. Take long walks in the fields or on the beach. You like a glass of wine. You like the Beatles. People choose a lot of different things. And sometimes things just happen. Beep. Beep. Beep.

The number's higher now. Of little crosses. A little boy. His name was Patrick. He was only twelve and walking home. They reckon that the driver was asleep. She was a junior doctor, young herself. Her life's ruined now, says Leanne. You agree and drink your Nescafé in plastic sippy cups for health and safety. You can't be drinking mugs around the kids. It doesn't taste the same. But coffee's coffee.

You wonder, as the beeping punctuates the radio, if someone's there beside you. Or maybe a variety of some-ones, depending on the day. The car feels different when the beeping's there. Not different-bad. Just different.

The air is charged with something. You had assumed it was your own frustration. An inability to figure out what's going on and stop it. Why had you expected you could do that? You never could. You never did before.

Heavy's how you feel most mornings anyway. Your feet find it harder to step out of the car, to walk to work, unlock the door and turn on all the lights and start pre-paring. Flick on the heating. Make a cup of tea. The little chairs and all the little tables. You spend your whole day stooping, hurt your back.

The low thrum of the beep beep beep. You drive back to the spot, it doesn't stop. You drive away; you keep on driving till your petrol's down to dregs and gasps. The needle in the red you pull into Applegreen's. Get a danish. Get a cup of tea and fill the tank. When you start up, the beeping's stopped again and you're relieved.

Is it someone, was it someone once? Can you feel any-thing beyond a beep? It isn't all that different. Colder maybe. You are always cold though. It is spring, but you still wear a scarf, a winter coat. The winter mild, the bit-terness stings now at hands and feet through cheap acrylic gloves and sleeves and socks.

It's hard to sleep at night. The house is small but too big for one person. Getting out of bed to check locked doors, to switch off lights. It isn't that you're lonely. It's just a lot. Living is a lot of little jobs and big ones and sometimes they all coalesce in front of you. You can't see past them really. It's like a hill that's full of slippy mud and brittle rocks. You knew that it was big but now it's dangerous. You need to get some sleep. You wake up thinking thoughts.

Leanne meets with you about a child. He's gluten-free and stealing others' sandwiches. She says it is a health risk. He's so quick though. Does it flying. Does it when your back is turned. He's coming home with tummy pains a lot. His mother has complained. He's only three. He doesn't have the sense to not be stealing. It's up to you to stop him doing that, she says.

She writes it in her little yellow book and you want to ask her what she's writing down but you do not. It's about you. Collecting bits of you she doesn't like to offer up when you ask for a raise, ask for time off. You rarely ask for things but you still want them. You work so hard. You tell her you work hard; she says I know.

Her hair is highlighted, her chin a little point like someone filed it. She has cheekbones, Leanne. Dresses well. Her earrings match her top. You hate your jeans. Your lap two draught excluders shoved together. Bulging as black pudding. Marked with stains. Fromage frais and poster paint and sand. Her and Paula thick as thieves and you do all the work. You should be running the place. You almost do already. No one likes you. No one wants you here. And if you left, where would you go at your age?

After work, it's hard to start the car. Your hands keep shaking when you think of Leanne's little voice. So diplomatic. Telling you these things as if you didn't know. You made a poster when the kids went home. Their little faces gathered all together, and a little stalk with a green leaf poking out. A grape bunch of kids. You think it's funny. What if it is not? What if there's something in it she could scribble in her yellow book? You try to warp it, try to find an angle. But you can't. It doesn't mean she won't.

You loved your little house when you first moved. Because it was all yours. It wasn't pretty but you'd paint the walls. You'd put up pictures, pay a man to come and fix the bathrooms. Have a dado rail put up in the hall. It suits you now, the shape of it. The colour. That doesn't mean you like it or it's nice.

No beeping on the way home and you stop. Pull in beside the sign and slam on the emergency triangle. You sit there, waiting. Thinking. Just in case.

A little photo of the little boy. A votive candle stand filled up with rain. So many flowers piled on top of flowers. Primroses and pansies, a baldy gang of hyacinths in a pot. You love the smell of hyacinths in the springtime. And maybe there's something the mechanic could do to switch the button off. Just stop the beeping altogether. Then you'd be done with it. You wrap your legs inside the car again and turn the key and make your way back home. You boil some ravioli for your tea.

Your mother felt much better right before. She smiled at you. She asked about your brother. Where he was. He'd gone back to Australia you told her. It wasn't true. He was asleep in your guest bedroom, phone on loud and waiting for a call. You don't know why that lie came out your mouth. She smiled at you. At least I have my little girl, she said. My daughter. She held your hand. And when her eyes flicked closed again you rang him. She was dead before he hit the road.

Days pass and sometimes there is beeping. Sometimes not. You approach expecting it to start and when it comes it's almost a relief. It's happened and you don't need to be scared. Just wait it out. It will be over soon. You hold your breath a little as you near the sign. The text and the black hole. Proceed with caution. How else would you though? It's all you know.

You watch your soaps. You make enough lasagne for the week. Freeze half of it. It's handy to have in. Cooking for one person's hard, they say, but you don't think so. The only one you have to please is yourself. And if you're tired you can leave the dishes.

Leanne is engaged. A little nicer, showing off her ring and booking things, researching different venues, different looks. She doesn't want to leave it for too long. A year's the max, she says. The limit. It was buy a house or plan a wedding. So they'll stay put till they're good and married in their fancy apartment. Her fiancée's got some big finance job. They've been together since she was fifteen. You get the kids to make her paper cards. Blobs in dresses. Little soft red hearts. It's nice to do a kind thing for somebody. She posts the best one on her profile page.

In the car on the way home you turn the radio up, right up. The music's louder, louder than the news and weather. Louder than the rain upon the glass. There are loose chippings on the road this evening. You can hear them crunching underwheel like bone.

Shifting fifth to fourth and fourth to third and down to second for the turn. You learned to drive when you were just a kid. Your mother taught you and she drove you mad. Telling you to look when you were looking. Rolling eyes as engine spluttered out. She wanted you to have your independence. And now you do. There's nothing tying you to anything. The house is just a house. The job's a job. The children would be fine, you know, without you. Horsing gluten into their hungry mouths.

The rain is hard and soft and all at once. It makes the night look fiercer. The trees are budding green and skeletal above the car. The little corpses on the motorway. Cats and rats and foxes. Hard when they're all squashed to tell what's what.

The beeping when it starts is low, insidious. You do not notice it until the turn, but as you do, you're conscious that it's been there for a while. Since you passed by the spot. It took your mother just a week to die. But on the road it varies. Cars can do all kinds of things to bodies. Pulverize or dent them, scrape or scar. The impact of a human skull on things. On wheels and tarmacadam.

You heard about a man who lost his mind. Not the way you'd think. Acquired brain injury, you've heard it called. He had a wife and children and afterwards he couldn't count his fingers. An accountant. And he remembered what he was before. Why can't I do this now, he'd ask, why don't you like me? You think they later put him in a home.

It would be hard to live beside a ghost. Something asking questions out like that. Reminding you of things you should forget or put aside. Dead, but not yet dead. And always asking.

You're turning up your driveway.

Beep beep beep.

You're parking at your house.

It isn't stopping.

Gentle little light and beep beep beep.

You click your seat belt off. You sit there for a long time, in the driveway between the house and road. Your hand is on the key in the ignition. The noise is there and still it isn't stopping. You do not want to turn the engine off. And then you do, and walk into the night.

You're not alone.

Little Lives

JOANNE
Unknown brand, head and arms vinyl, 1950s.

Cloth (cotton) body stuffed with unknown substance, possibly a sort of putty, indented to the touch. Difficult to reshape, but can be done if left in direct sunlight and gently massaged.

Three visible holes on right side of neck, scratch across eye, discoloration and staining on the torso. All fingers and toes present. May have contained a squeaker at one time, but doesn't now.

Some loose-hanging threads. Do not snip or remove, she doesn't like it. Though a baby, this doll is possessed of an older spirit, possibly inhuman in origin. Flickering lights, blown fuses, and a clicking sound not unlike the mandibles of something very large may disturb. May move when not in your eye-line, but never very far.

Joanne would do well as an introductory haunted doll, however, due to the inhuman nature of what is inside her, caution is recommended. Will not get along with children or pets (one fatality, possibly unrelated).

Asking Price: €450.00, plus shipping.

Photographs available on request, but Joanne may not grant permission, and with so many little lives in one location, I must respect their wishes. Contact via website, or Joanne directly through the medium of your choosing.

SERIOUS BUYERS ONLY. I AM SICK OF TIME WASTERS.

Will not accept international buyers for this one.

1.

Beside every doll, we keep a list. Sometimes it's a collection of old envelopes, brown to bright, and other times it is on coloured cue cards, as though the little legs would straighten up, approach a podium and give a speech in someone else's voice. Some charges require notebooks right away, or scrapbooks where the histories have grown too long for bullet points.

2.

Sometimes newspaper articles are pasted in, apparently at random. Fires, drownings, deaths. Calamity. Calamity. Calamity.

3.

I started dusting the shelves the first time Mam got sick and had no energy. She hates to dust so now it's just my job. I clean them one by one, with special solutions, recipes my granny handed down. To keep some instincts dampened, recharge false skin, polish glass eyes, small shoes.

4.

The miniature clothing is not for the washing machine. We handwash it carefully. Small white cotton socks, flamenco dresses. Some things can't be cleaned, and others shouldn't. Certain stains increase an item's value – semen, blood. Tears are harder to identify. They don't yellow a thing like old, dark sweat.

5.

Some dolls collect stains under armpits, as though they have been wearing themselves for years – soft, pale, stuffed bodies. As though they're ready for another venture. They might be still for months, or maybe years. But something always happens in the end.

6.

A little pulse.

A blink.

A dash of spite.

Or something far less tangible than that. A sharp internal stirring. A sense of something you can't put your big meat-finger on. An almost-story waiting to be told.

7.

When I was a little girl I was still bigger than a doll. I liked the story Thumbelina because of that phrase 'no bigger than a thumb'. I wanted to be so small it would define me. I always took up space though. Sometimes too much space and I was punished. Scratches on my soft skin in the dark. Little pinches leaving little scars.

They are.

Unruly things.

They are.
Important.

8.

You can convince yourself of anything. I saw this thing online about shared delusions. Psychosomatic illness. People's bodies hurting them because they suppress trauma. And I wondered if it could be that, with some of the people we get the dolls from. The part of themselves they don't want to look at going inside plastic, china, wood. Becoming something other, something else.

9.

I mean we all have things.

10.

Melissa's aunt had a psychosomatic illness, and it got so bad that she couldn't do her job, and ended up using a wheelchair, even though no scan could diagnose what was wrong with her. Eventually the doctors thought that it was the death of her brother and that was fine, but she was still in pain. She needed help and never got the right kind. Now she uses crutches, which is progress I suppose.

11.

I saw a flash of a film on TV when I was babysitting once, and there was this image of a woman suspended on a butcher's hook. I flicked away. I don't like unhappy things or scary stories. I don't want to escape to something worse. I want a girl who is seen by someone or something kind. I want someone like me, and I want her to be okay at the beginning and a little sad or angry in the middle and then happy by the end.

I want a shining face to look at her and want her.
A face that's made of flesh with jelly eyes.

12.

I don't know how much Mam believes about the dolls.
She says there's money in them, and while there's
money in them we'll keep doing them. We have ones
whose stories we can trace, through years, through fires,
bankruptcy, murders and breakdowns. But she's always
going to car boot sales as well. Or searching on the internet for the dolls that look like they've been haunted. The
china ones with big dark eyes, and maybe a little crack
that trails right down the centre of their face, so they
look damaged. People think that damaged things can
hurt them.

13.

Maybe we can.

14.

We have a no-refund policy. But that doesn't mean no
returns. We'll always take returns. We can sell them on no
bother, and we share the emails with the names redacted to
back up how haunted the doll is. I thought about staining
them with tea like we do other documents but it doesn't
work for email because email isn't as old-timey as a newspaper clipping from forty years ago, or a photograph from
the civil war.

15.

Sometimes we get phone calls, or desperate emails beg-
ging us to come, please come to a house and collect a
doll. And when we do, Mam goes. We've driven down

boreens and back roads in our dressing gowns in the middle of the night. To get to them before they think to charge us.

16.

Sometimes it's one we didn't even sell them in the first place.

17.

Once, on the way back from a fairly normal-looking house in town, Mam turned to me, and said, 'Sarah, that wasn't the doll.'

And she shivered. Something in her face I'd never seen.

The doll in the back of the car with Cupid's bow lips and one eye missing.

They'd done that to her. Inside the house.

We all like to take things out on someone.

18.

Mam generally makes up the backstories when we don't get them first-hand. She has a voice recorder on her phone, and a Dictaphone as well, the kind that journalists used to use, she says. She's not sure if they use them any more. We don't know any journalists. I keep track of the stories, and file them with the dolls, adding in photographs sometimes. If they're going to America, I can use photographs of the abandoned farmhouse on the land near where we live with the odd made-up one. But we can't use them around here, because everybody knows the story of what happened there and why no one will go inside it now.

19.

It's useful, Mam says, because if anyone was to come asking, no one would say a word about it and sure couldn't it have been a haunted doll?

20.

You can take a lot of photos in there, and depending on what angle you use, it looks like a completely different place. And there's a lot to like. I've left dolls strewn in the fireplace. On top of the cracked Sacred Heart. Hanging limply from the big nail in the middle of the wall. Or standing to attention in the corner. There's one window that looks out on the wilderness of what used to be the Mahons' land before. Another window, differently shaped, looks out on the pools of water and bogland and the hills behind. I've also done one through the cracked ribcage of the roof, but you have to be careful because crows roost up in the tall old trees and the floor is spattered with their shit and it could go in your eye very easily.

21.

And from the other side you can see the hedgerow and the dirt path and the corner of our house. If there is washing on the line you can't see the window. But if there isn't you can. I don't like using that one. But sometimes you have to for variety. We live pretty far from anyone, our closest neighbours are Karl and Davey Mahon, but they're a twenty-minute walk up the road and they don't like Mam at all.

22.

Mam also buys old books for authenticity. You can use the paper to make old documents. Lots of books have a few blank pages either side and you can rip them out, or pull out a page covered in words but splatter ink over most of the words so it just says something spooky like 'God Help Us'.

I find blotting out words soothing. It feels like magic, changing what they mean.

23.

Mam likes to make up rules. And set limits. She says it encourages people to break them. When we say 'no international buyers', a lot of the time someone international will think we'll break that rule for them if they shell out way more money. We go back and forth, but they're usually right. We got a grand for an old Skipper doll once. She had her feet gnawed off. I think she might have even been mine.

24.

I don't really understand why people want them. Why would you buy a problem, or a lie?

25.

Mam makes up rules for me sometimes as well. I have to have my homework done before I get my dinner. This doesn't apply if I get more than an hour and a half of homework because dinner is always at seven. She also doesn't want me getting any tattoos on my arms because she has three and it can be difficult when she's trying to seem like different pairs of arms throughout the dolls' history.

26.

We have a lot of dress-up clothes. Car boot sales are great for them. And estate sales, which always make Mam angry.

Because of the English. But they're well worth going to, unless you get someone else who's into dolls. Which a lot of people are, apparently.

27.

Sometimes my friends want to come and visit and I bring them over, and they always look at the big door with the symbols on it that says 'DO NOT ENTER' and sometimes they want to go in there, and sometimes they just ask about it. If I need to go out to take in a wash, or look for the cat, they always come out too 'for company'. And I pretend I don't know they're afraid.

28.

I do let them in if they ask. But not right away, and I make them work for it.

Like an international buyer.

29.

She touched my face. She told me that it was dangerous to be a pretty child.

30.

She touched my face.

29.

Sometimes we make tinctures and solutions from my grandmother's recipes. Mam says that she was an auld bitch but that she knew what she was doing with these lads. She means the dolls. We put vodka, ragwort, garlic, ash and fingernails into the bottle. And TCP as well. We bury it outside for six days and six nights and then we dig it up and then it's ready. We use glass jars to bury it but we put it into a spray bottle before we use it because it's handier.

28.

Most of them won't do anything to you. But you have to be careful. A bit like men, Mam says.

27.

We got a new one.
   It has a tongue.
   It's weird.

26.

It licked me and I giggled but it wasn't very funny and then I couldn't stop laughing and Mam slapped me and made me a cup of tea with lots of sugar in it and said that we mightn't have any friends over until this one sells, love, and I said fair enough because it was.

25.

Mam isn't happy. The thing with her womb is back, and her hair is falling out from the stress of it. She wants it gone but if she goes to hospital again I'll be here alone and there are a few of them we have to sell before that happens.

24.

I pulled my jumper over my face but it kept moving closer. I could see it moving through the spaces in the wool that let in light.
   One step at a time.

23.

Granny was a normal granny, really. She made great bread. She just liked dolls. And if you have more than a hundred dolls some of them are bound to be haunted. So, she learned ways to mind them. Knowing about them helped her to keep track. She wouldn't have sold any of them if she was still alive, but she wouldn't have minded Mam doing it. She might be glad that she has any sort of job. She didn't have much faith in her.

22.

Mam says that I can be anything I want to be, and she can pay for me to go to college in Dublin or Galway or somewhere else no bother. When I'm finished school, I should go off and live my life and follow my dreams.

21.

I dreamed of a wide white mouth with flat black teeth. There was a sheen on them that was almost golden but it wasn't gold it might have been dirt it might have been dirt it might have been dirt.

20.

She doesn't often bury things in graveyards but I could smell the grave dirt on her hands it doesn't smell like muck it smells like mass.

19.

Little pink tongue the same shape and size as mine but softer and more moist.

Slick.

AURELIA
Bisque doll, German, 1860s. (RARE)

Aurelia is a find for any collector, even without her backstory. Her skin is unpolished porcelain and has a matte texture. If you look at the reference photo, you'll see that she has four perfect little teeth beneath her top lip. Her body is made of porcelain and not the usual cloth and she is anatomically correct.

She was brought here by a Polish child who settled in Ireland in the aftermath of the Second World War, and was confiscated by the Daughters of Charity of Saint Vincent de Paul. From there she ended up in a Magdalene Laundry, where more than a hundred bodies were found buried in a field out the back. We cannot guarantee she had anything to do with it but I wouldn't be surprised. She has bitten me twice now and the wounds refuse to heal. We can always smell burning hair when she is in the room. Minimal injury so far, but there is a sense of menace and danger in the house since she arrived and therefore she is PRICED TO SELL.

Aurelia would be suitable for a sole collector, or a large family where no one would be left alone in the house with her. She would make a charming addition to a museum of the occult, or an interesting subject for a paranormal investigation. NO VIEWINGS. SERIOUS BUYERS ONLY.

Photographs of Aurelia and the bite marks are included below. She moved once while I was taking them but I couldn't say for sure that it was preternatural movement. I might have jostled her and not clocked it.

Price available on request. To be clear, it is a four-figure sum I'm after for Aurelia.

International buyers welcome but shipping is at your own expense. I'm not made of money.

18.

I did that one, I think it's pretty good. We got her in Age Action but she is a real antique, so she cost us twenty euro.

17.

Mam asked me if I'd rather be here alone or would she get someone to stay but she doesn't have many friends and I knew it would be hard so I said it'd be fine. I can look after myself. Run the business. Cook dinners. The only thing I can't do is drive, but only because I'm too young. She's going to get a taxi there and back. I'll go with her for the first bit and then I'll meet Melissa and them in town and maybe one of their parents will drop me home. It's a really simple procedure. They scoop it out and then they do a biopsy. Sometimes it goes away without any treatment and sometimes it gets worse. The last time they sent her home the same day but it's more complicated this time. Too many at once, and all together. She'll definitely be gone for one day and probably for two. I'm not religious but I keep thinking about the bit out of the Hail Mary about the fruit of your womb. I imagine it like that, apricots and grapes all growing in her. She should just get the whole thing taken out, but she doesn't have to yet, and doesn't want to. When it's really, really bad they don't give you a choice, I think, like with my appendix, so maybe it will all be fine. She goes in for ultrasounds and says it's just like with a baby but instead of a baby there's something else growing in there and it's not as nice. But if you didn't know, and saw the shape, you could almost think it was a little person tucked inside.

16.

Like us and not like us and isn't that what's weird about the dolls. That they're shaped like people but aren't people. That's why we put the dark parts of ourselves inside them. Our crimes and our disasters. The energy. It doesn't just appear. It comes from us.

15.

I try to be calm but I have to go into the toilets of McDonald's and have a cry and they all know there's something going on but they don't ask. Melissa's mum doesn't offer me a lift, so I have to get two buses and walk for an hour and a half and by the time I'm home I'm just wiped out, and there's nothing from Mam so I make myself beans on toast and light the fire, read the internet and fall asleep.

TIMOTHY
Tiny Tim Doll, vinyl, 1990s.

Face melted slightly. Tiny Tim is a doll that can drink water and then urinate to train children how to change nappies. Unfortunately sometimes the water that emerges has an acrid stench (possibly useful for cursework). We were asked to remove Tiny Tim from a house in Carlow, where he had caused havoc (scans of their handwritten testimony included below). They had a druid in afterwards to cleanse it and have had no trouble since. Tim has been quite placid since he arrived here, but sometimes around him we can hear small chirps, of the sort a cat makes upon sighting a bee on the windowsill. We cannot guarantee that paranormal activity will occur with Timothy, and are therefore willing to sell to a family with children or pets. He does not seem to dislike animals and my daughter has had no trouble with him. He enjoys being taken off the shelf and handled, and is in better form if this is done often. If you really want to annoy him, leave him alone in his box for a week or two and something bad will probably happen.

We're letting Timothy go for €35.00 (plus shipping), but we will also be accepting higher offers.

14.

I ring the hospital.

13.

I get some messages from Melissa and them, asking me if I'm okay, after the crying, and I don't respond because I don't know what to say – it all depends on Mam and how she is.

12.

She isn't coming home again tonight. It took more out of her than they thought it would or they had to take more out of her than they thought they would, or something like that. I couldn't really understand what she was saying. Her voice was far away and different than it usually is.

11.

I packed up Sophie, Laura and Imogen to go to the post office. I can't ask one of the neighbours to give me a lift. I don't want them to know I'm here alone.

10.

I think I might not like people the way that other people like people. Romantically I mean, but also in the other way. They're such hard work.

9.

If anything were to happen to Mam, I don't know where I'd go. I couldn't stay here, not all by myself. People need people, for life stuff, and for company as well. Even Karl Mahon has Davey, like.

8.

I went in to clean the shelves and of course they were everywhere and I had to set them all back and open all the boxes and check that they were in the right order. It took a while. I listened to a podcast about sharks. People think that all sharks are bad, but no sharks are, not really.

Some just end up eating humans.

We eat other animals all the time.

They don't sell little chunks of us to other sharks to make money.

They just get hungry.

Everyone gets hungry now and then.

7.

My phone lost all its battery in the dolls' room, and I'd been there for seven hours when I left. I don't remember anything after the podcast. And that was only fifty minutes long. I hate it when that happens.

6.

I sprayed and locked the door and put Sophie, Laura and Imogen out on the porch and locked the front door on them. They don't do anything once they're all wrapped up. But I wanted to be careful.

5.

I went to sleep and when I woke up there was a loud knocking on the door and it was shaking the walls and it was like someone had their two fists against it and they were thumping, thumping and yelling, and I looked out and it was our neighbour Karl and he looked angry so I closed the curtains and left him at it. He was saying something but I couldn't make out the words, it was like there was a pool of water or a cloud between his voice and my ears. I splashed my face with water and checked the time and when I turned my phone on, Mam had been trying to get through to me, and I thought maybe it was about that so I opened the door but it wasn't that at all he wanted it was something else.

4.

I don't know how he knew I was alone.

3.

Mam called to say that she was discharged and so I went and got her in a taxi. It wasn't very practical, but I really wanted to see her.

2.

Someone bought Mabel, so we don't have to worry about money for a while. Mabel is in a newspaper clipping from 1927 where she levitates in front of a startled girl in a little pinafore. The girl's eyes are wide and Mabel's face is just like Mabel's face, all calm and blue-eyed. Mam was tired but she said they got it out and it shouldn't be back again, not for ages – we got five whole years last time. And wasn't I a great girl.

1.

Her scarf smelled like roses and disinfectant. Her breath was stale.

0.

And didn't I do well.

Appointment

Eimear waits in the chair. The hygienist (nurse? She introduced herself as 'Claire') has left the room to get something. The walls are cream. The chair is wipe-clean fabric. They always are; it wouldn't make much sense for them not to be. Through the blind she can see the light, little patches of colour moving, stopping. The ceiling is high, and there is cornicing without a single strand of spiderweb. The lino is spotless, even though it's the last appointment of the day. (Is there a secret mop, all tucked away?)

That's what Eimear does in these places. Looks for dirt. Amounts of damage, disrepair. The comfort of decay. She peers down at her feet, small and tilted one towards the other, like awkward friends. Her runners are a little scuffed, she realizes. Her heels are nicer, but they're in her bag. She walked here (and she could have changed, she could have put them on but they are getting her money already and do people do that? Dress up for the dentist?). Her nails are done. Her teeth are clean. She's brushed them four times today. Flossed last night and all. But she can taste the onion from the salad on her breath. She should have chosen something else instead. Onion doesn't let your mouth forget.

Claire is back. She is examining. Eimear opens her mouth and lets the wiry implement travel from tooth to tooth, gum to gum.

'Does this hurt?' Claire asks.

Eimear tells her no, but it's uncomfortable. She doesn't know where to put her tongue. Right or left or back towards her throat. When she was younger, she used to worry about swallowing her tongue, late at night. It lives inside your mouth, but you don't think about it, and when you are asleep, what is to stop you sucking it right down inside your throat and the fat meat of it stopping your windpipe? She would lie awake wondering about that, and in the morning dark lines under eyes and off to school. You can't predict what happens when you're conscious, but you have more control. More *something*.

Claire begins the clean, the little spit-suck thing that tastes like mint, the whirring yoke. It's not a drill, but the sting of it on teeth. The tinny sound. Eimear feels an eyelash on her cheek. A spider's leg. A tiny little weight, thick with mascara. She wants to move her hand to brush it off but she holds still. Her shoulders tight against the dentist's chair.

Claire has nice eyebrows. Small but thickly shaped. Her cheekbones are dotted with freckles and Eimear can't find any blackheads on her skin. They're rarer on adults; when she was a teenager almost everybody had a speckle. She wonders now if it is only her. Claire's shoulders slope a little and her breasts are small. She looks like she runs. Eimear can picture her in proper gym gear. Lululemon, tight in on the abs. Eimear goes to the gym, in little sleeveless tops or baggy t-shirts. Nothing to indicate she's good at this. Nothing that says *look*. (The gym's a scary place; there are so many things you can forget to bring. Shampoo, a spare pair of socks, a lock, your little swipe card. And when you're in, there are more ways to fail. Someone beside you on the treadmill, running, running. Hair swept up perfectly. Other women know how to do things.)

Claire removes the thing that's not a drill. 'That's the worst bit over.'

'I didn't mind.' Eimear's voice is thin. Her fingers still. The eyelash is still there. Claire moves her finger towards her face, and Eimear flinches.

'Sorry, sorry,' Claire says. 'I don't know why I did that.'

'It's okay. The eyelash. I could feel it.' Eimear tries to ease the tension in her body, in the room. 'I wanted to myself but I didn't know if I was allowed to move.'

'If it happens again, just flap your hand a bit,' Claire tells her. 'We want our patients comfortable here.'

Their eyes meet for a moment and it is a gentle thing. A kindness, Eimear thinks. A little kindness. It almost makes her cry. It's been so long. And what would fingers on her cheek feel like?

Her mother doesn't hug her any more. She doesn't like to be touched now. She doesn't, half the time, remember who Eimear is. She calls her other names. Names of people who've made a deeper impact. Loved and hated names: Margaret, Leah. Anne. She asks for her other children. She never asks for Eimear.

Eimear runs her tongue along her teeth. She rinses out her mouth. She spits. She rinses and she spits again. Then washes her hands in the sink.

'Thank you,' she says.

And Claire tells her she's welcome and she's sorry. Excuse her for the … She does not know why.

'It's quite all right.' Eimear's voice is formal.

She leaves and pays the lady at reception.

Back into her heels and back to work.
Her smile is very clean.

All evening at the desk she runs her tongue over her teeth. Clean. It wasn't her that caused the heart attack. The things her mother says. They aren't true. It's the anger talking. The frustration. Where she is, and all that she has lost. Eimear thinks about the lost things too. The little choices. You focus on your career, assume that the right person will just find you. And then you realize that when you are a woman on your own, it doesn't matter, really, what you want. Liam is off in London, Joe has kids, and so does Leah. Eimear only lived across the town, sure. It wasn't much to ask. Or not as much as it would be, for them. She doesn't have as many things to do. Her life is smaller, lesser. She knew they thought that, even before. Something in the syrup of a tone. Inside their voices, eyes. Spinster face. As though she were a child. They couldn't, in good conscience, have put their mother in a home. Besides, they were expensive. They pay for help twelve hours a week, and Eimear does the rest. She could see it coming several miles away, but couldn't do a thing to stave it off. At first, they were going to make a roster. Give her a break. But then she rented out her own apartment and they felt that meant it was a paid position.

She drives by her old place sometimes. You can't see in the window from the road and she wouldn't be annoying the new tenant – the letting agency takes care of that. But she finds the window, counting up across, and she imagines another her still in there. Unaware of what is going on. Calmly living life. Deciding things. It makes her heart widen in an uncomfortable way, to think of that. It isn't healthy though. The road not taken is the road that kills you.

106

At Christmas, she roasted the turkey. Cooked it all, for all of them together. Liam, Leah, Mario, Joanne and little Íde. Joe eats with Breda's people. In the North. She sat in front of the television afterwards, until Leah pointedly began to do the washing up. As if it were a massive favour. As if their company should have been enough. Eimear got up to help her, because everything was being bashed so angrily, and they ended up screaming.

'I'm not the help,' Eimear yelled at her. 'I'm not the fucking help.'

'No one said you were,' Leah snapped. 'You martyr. We all have our own lives.'

'And I don't?'

'You've more time to be selfish even minding her than I do in the week.'

'You chose your kids. I didn't choose this here.'

And her face crumpled up. 'God forgive you.'

'God doesn't need to forgive me.' Eimear scowled. 'I'm not your servant. And I am not going to have this put on me.'

Leah started to cry. 'I dreaded coming here. I dreaded it.'

Eimear's voice, meaner than she meant it, cut across her. 'You,' she said. 'You and your *anxiety*. And your *depression*. And your *self-care*. Where's my self-care? I have no time for it. You stole that from me. My life is Mam now. My whole life is work and Mam and work and Mam and work. And you wouldn't even let me put my feet up Christmas Day without a face on you.'

'What face did I have?' asked Leah. 'I can't help how I look. And why is this my fault all of a sudden?'

The lads turned up the television to try and drown them out. It didn't work. Liam popped his head through the doorway after a while. 'We can hear ye in there. The kids and Mam can hear ye.'

Eimear closed her eyes and shut her mouth. She inhaled deeply, and began to scoop submerged food remnants from the plughole. There was always more work to be done. She only had two days off. Leah was a housewife. And that was labour too, Eimear knew it was. But she was right today.

They scrubbed and dried in silence. And when Liam knocked to say Mam needed changing, Eimear glared and Leah scuttled out.

That night, putting her into her nightclothes, pulling soft cotton over wrinkled skin, Mam asked, 'Am I that bad?'

And Eimear told her no, and that she was okay now. And both those things were true but not for long. Months passed and Mam was getting crosser, meaner. Eimear found her teenage self again. The anger at the person that she'd come from. She worked remotely as much as they allowed. And the work got done and she was still good at it. She knew her stuff. She hadn't gotten where she was by not knowing. She thought of Other Eimear through the window, booking holidays. Going out without arranging care. Taking long hot showers, sleeping well.

Eimear finds herself avoiding mirrors. She doesn't like the feel of her own eyes.

It's fine. It's fine. She's fine. She has clean teeth. She's booked a nail appointment for next week, and maybe hair the Wednesday after that. You need to carve out space. To force yourself to dress up like a person. But every day another layer is peeling off her heart. As thin as film. The exhaustion of keeping up with the little jobs. With parenting your parent. Making sure she's clean. That there aren't any food stains on her top. That she hasn't eaten all the biscuits Eimear hides inside the press with the child lock on it. She breaks in with a dexterity she doesn't have for other things. Eimear doesn't remember Mam having such a passion for biscuits when she was growing up. But now they're like a feed of pints was for Dad. She'll cram as many as possible into her mouth and not feel full until she knows they're gone. All of them gone.

Is that what old age is? Eimear can feel it, see it on her body. It's encroaching. Her back acts up. Her skin is looser. Not so you would notice, but she sees it. Is it first the skin, the neck, the back and then the brain? Mam was healthy until she wasn't. It started slow and then came all at once. Dad was more sudden. Heart attack in the back garden. She'd been twenty-five, and she remembers Liam on the phone to her. He rang her and he yelled at her. The voice-mail: 'He's dying, dying, Eim, why aren't you here?'

His voice was very broken, very young. And being there would not have changed the death, but Liam always liked to have someone to blame. Made him feel a bit more in control. It's hard to be beside the end of things. And Dad was great, he had the strongest voice. The biggest heart. Of course, Eimear knew, he would have judged her. They all would have. She kept it to herself. The other life.

She'd been in London when he keeled over. Of course, when she got home it was too late. She'd listened to Liam's voice after the appointment. And then excused herself, gone to the ladies. Vomited. Twice. Tidied up. Proceeded to the airport. Sorted a flight. She'd bled for days and days and told nobody. The closest she had come. To being a mother. She didn't want a small dependent thing. She'd never even had a cat, a dog. A guinea pig. So many little lives she didn't want, and suddenly she found she was inside one. (This wasn't her. This woman wasn't her.)

Mam wants to go to the solicitor in town. Rejig her will. 'I'll make sure everybody's taken care of,' she mutters. 'Not like my own father, God rest his soul.'

Her hands trace the sign of the cross. Eimear's eyes close. Someone died on that. A lot of someones. (What if it had been a noose, an axe? A little jar of poison? What shapes would hands make then to think of God?) Still, sometimes Eimear finds her heathen lips tracing a soft Hail Mary. The time it takes gives her the space to breathe.

'Okay, Mam,' Eimear says. Her face is flat. Mam often wants to change her will. But she isn't competent. At first, Eimear used to argue with her about it. Now she shuts up and hopes that she forgets. If she persists, Eimear will send her to the office. They know her well. Their families connect. Too tired. Too tired for another row. She runs her tongue across her gleaming teeth.

'They didn't like me. My own parents. In the end. They didn't …' Tears stream down her face, snail trail lodging in the wrinkles. 'It all went to the boys. I *minded* them, and then …'

'It's okay, Mam.'

'You're my child. And I don't think you love me anymore. It isn't fair.'

'I love you,' Eimear tells her. 'I do love you.'

She offers her a biscuit with her tea.

She changes Mam into her nightdress, ignoring the grumbles of 'I can do it myself.' It's true, she can, but it takes so much time. At first, Eimear was better at waiting. At letting. At giving of herself. At first, there was more there of her to give. Now she's just looking forward to bed. It's the best part of the day. When it's over. Under the duvet with her hot-water bottle, reading or scrolling through her phone. That's reading too, but faffier. (They say that you should turn off screens in bed. That you'll sleep better. But it is hard to calm a racing brain. And when she's by herself … It used to be recharging, but now the thoughts cloud in. The what-am-I, what-is-this. She has to force them out to sleep at all. So, the routine.)

The following morning, she's waiting for Mam beside the shower when she emerges, nude, and starts to yell at her about the heart attack. About the trip.

'On holidays you said. You weren't on holidays. We knew what you were at. It would have been the first grandchild. And don't you look at me like that. Don't you dare. The face on you.'

And Eimear holds the towel out and she wraps her mother in it. They've had this chat before. No need to prolong it. She dries her, roughly (not too roughly though). Her skin is thin. She applies cream to little cracks of eczema, to ulcers.

'Did Dad know?'

'He knew what you were at while he was dying,' her mam snaps. 'I found out and I told him what you were.'

'And what am I?'

Eimear asks again, again.

'What am I?'

The answer never comes.

She gets the brush, the hairdryer.

'Don't put me near the mirror. I don't like it.'

'I won't, Mam,' Eimear says. 'I won't. I won't.'

She takes her time so hair won't snag from scalp. She holds her breath. In the reflection, she sees both their heads from the side: one shiny dyed, one silver, almost blue. Four eyes, the same blue colour, all resigned. (Is that where ghosts live, lurking in the spaces – who you were before and who you are now?)

Eimear shakes the thought off, plucks stray hairs from the brush, rolls them up like tumbleweed and bins them. Birds could use them for their little nests, she thinks, thread silver through their houses. Dad used to tell them stories about that. About the cleverness of wild creatures, and all the bits of them that could be used. Mam's hair is soft, and even when she's cross she smells like comfort. (If I were small, things would be easier. If I were less like her, less like myself.)

'Do I look nice, Leah?' asks her mother.

'I'm not Leah.'

'Who are you then?' Consternation flickers across her face.

'I'm here to help you,' Eimear says. 'Let's go to town, we'll walk around the shops, take tea.'

'Pop inside the church and light a candle?'

'If you like.'

Mam smiles. They face the day. In the car, Eimear feels a little bit of toast against her gum. (She needs to floss, before she brushes this evening. Her gums will bleed. But it will do her good.)

The smell of slurry through the open window. Her mother makes a face.

'It will be over soon. Just hold your breath.'

They make eye contact in the rear-view mirror, and wait. Until they're sure it's safe and even past that. Small motes of dust are clinging to the dashboard. The road to town is wide, the air is clean.

Spar.

Fahy's.

The post office.

Appointment

There are so many places here, to be. But still, the car drives past her old apartment. She counts the grey rectangles. Licks her teeth. (Is living it what makes a life a life?) The traffic moves, her mother smiles at her and Eimear's lips curl back. They go to town.

Skein

It takes time for anything to grow. You come out needing and you grow up wanting. The seed of something wrong was always in me. Waiting, in my flesh, for one small click.

Growing up, I really liked attention. 'Look at me,' I'd scream out, 'look at me'. My mother tells me a story like it's cute and not shameful: when I was a little girl, about nine or ten, I asked her to come with me into the bathroom, pulled down my knickers and presented her with my vulva. Hairs were growing on it and I didn't like it one bit. Mum couldn't do anything about my pubic hair, except tell me that she had it too, that it would keep on coming. Hers poked out the sides of her underwear, and was so thick and dark it obscured the shape and size of her genitals, like a veil.

Mine was not like that. It was patchy and troublesome, and the parts of myself I didn't like escaped from it like shameful little rashers. Sometimes, in a fit of sadness at the world, I would lie in bed at night, plucking out the new hairs one by one.

I worried a lot about what falling in love would feel like, and whether or not I'd meet someone before I turned fifteen. This was my cut-off age. I had a plan: in first love by fifteen, lose it to that as-yet faceless boy, break up before college, play the field, meet the one in third year, move in together for final year to play house, and then go travelling before the real world started. Maybe someone else after that, someone with a good job. That one I would marry.

As I grew, these plans came to nothing and I collected further things to hate. The shape and size of my nose, my forehead, breasts could be dissected by other girls, by anyone with eyes. My private parts were private, but I didn't really feel like they were mine either. There was a future boy who'd touch them and make me feel those romance-novel things.

My friend Maggie told me that I should be more sex-positive, sitting on my couch and watching our family dog hump a cushion as we milled through a tube of Pringles and a bag of jellies. Her parents were away for the weekend, so she was over at mine. Maggie had more guy friends than I did and she was always reading books about feminism even though she never left the house without a full face of makeup.

That summer, Maggie met a boy, Shane, while her family were on holidays in Roundstone. She dyed her hair purple and wore a lot less makeup, and she said it wasn't to do with him – it was to do with what she'd realized about *herself* through him, and I remember wanting a love like that, that would make me have more friends and be slightly cooler in the eyes of everyone. On Valentine's Day, he sent her a bunch of roses with the tops cut off to the school, and she laughed until the mascara got all smudged and stung her eyes.

A few of us went to Dublin on the train to meet Shane and his friends in Stephen's Green. We hung around and went to McDonald's. I had tried to look pretty, but I wasn't pretty, so no one really focused on me. Our quiet friend Sarah kissed a short, broad little dude with a barrel chest called Joseph, and I was jealous. Maggie and Shane went off for a couple of hours by themselves, and Sarah and myself went around Topshop and Urban Outfitters and all the vintage shops in Temple Bar. I bought a purple jumper with an elephant on it because I hoped that Maggie would think it was cool. I think I wore it twice. It was expensive, so I still have it, folded up somewhere.

When I went home that night, I took a shower and shaved my legs. I used a man's razor, not my dad's but one I'd bought for me after reading an article about how they were better for girls with sensitive skin because they were made for faces. I rubbed in grapefruit shower gel with little beads of red and purple in it, and I rinsed myself and peeled the hair off my body, and several layers of skin with it. The growth of it reminded me of when the lawn got redone, and we had to wait for the grass to come up. Soon, the grass was everywhere, and places it was not supposed to be – between the paving stones and amongst the dark blue gravel on our driveway. After my legs were done, I still felt too hairy, so I kept shaving. My pubic hair, my armpits, my arms, the little treasure trail of down between my navel and the beginning of my genitals. The hair that wasn't even hair, but I could see it sometimes when the light above the mirror caught my face. I tweezed the little buds as they cropped up.

Everything except my eyebrows and lashes.

I didn't want to be an alien, but I didn't want to be a woman either. Not unless I could be a really good one.

I wanted to feel smooth. Acceptable. I lay in bed that night and thought of Shane and Joseph, Connor and Paul and Saoirse. All of Maggie's new friends. I wasn't attracted to any of them, but I would have been with them if they had asked me. I wanted to be wanted.

Sometimes I met people who liked me and sometimes I liked them back and it was fine. We did things to each other. When I lost my virginity to another ex of Maggie's, Leon, it felt like he was breaking me in two. And he kept saying 'Do you want me to stop? Is this okay?' and I kept crying, crying and nodding and telling him to keep on going at it. I was behind schedule. This needed to get done. I closed my eyes and ground my teeth together till he finished.

He was kind, I think, but so freaked out he never messaged me again afterwards. My hair had grown back by that time, and I was fighting the parts of it I deemed totally unacceptable every time I shaved, sloughing off the extra skin and getting to work with a four-blade razor, called Renegade, for men who *work hard and play hard*.

I was working hard. It was my Leaving Cert year and everything felt high-stakes and troubling. My mother asked me once if I would like to see a counsellor, and I accused her of calling me mental and slammed the sitting-room door so hard the stained glass shattered. She made me come right back and sweep it up while she sellotaped a deconstructed cornflakes box to the hole I'd left in case any visitor cut their hands. The repairs came out of my pocket money.

After Leon, there was Gary Shaw. The boy who we always called by both his names, in the way that's done with boys who are more themselves than other boys. It's not a good thing, always, or a bad thing. It's just that there are some characters worth knowing. Gary Shaw was a pretty good GAA player. My dad knew who he was, which shouldn't have impressed me, but it did. He was a boy who was so good at things that his fame had spread to adults. His photograph was sometimes in the paper, sweaty and smiling surrounded by his teammates and once, by himself, running and cradling a ball, his face intent. I wanted him to look at me with that intensity. I tore the page out of the paper and stuck it in a scrapbook, though calling it a scrapbook would have disgusted me. I kept cinema stubs, stickers from apples and bananas I had eaten, beer mats and random things that I gathered up from other people's waste, like a magpie, unable to tell what was valuable and what was just a thing that shone.

I kept screenshots of clever things he'd said on my phone in a folder marked 'Geography Notes'. When he asked for my number, furtively, on the bus back from a night out in Moycullen, I wrote it down with a little pencil on fancy paper I'd gotten in a Christmas cracker instead of typing it into his phone. I was trying to be memorable but felt it came off weird in the end. It prolonged things. He folded it up and put it in his pocket, and when he got in touch, it was a friend request and not a message. His mam had put his cords through the wash and my number had been shredded.

Gary Shaw messaged me a lot, but we rarely met up. Sometimes I sent him pictures of my breasts. I usually put a little bit of blusher on the nipples, or pale-peach lipstick if I was stuck, but that was a bit too shiny and I worried he'd cop. Without a bit of help, they were more tan than pink and I wanted to be beautiful for him. If he shared my photo around, I wanted people to be turned on by it, not creeped out by my little brownish buttons, wrinkled from the cold. I worked so hard at being beautiful for Gary Shaw. At not demanding anything. Maggie told me I was being a fool. She liked alternative boys.

Boys who appreciated girls with anime badges on their bags.

But that was just another kind of trying. I didn't tell anyone about the photos we sent each other. He never put his face in his, and I don't think he put blusher on his dick. I wondered sometimes if it wasn't his, and later when I saw it in real life, I still couldn't be sure. Some of them are quite distinctive, but it would take a lot for me to pick one out of a line-up. He would tell me the things he wanted to do to me, and I would just agree to them. We had different groups of friends, and he never really wanted to see me by myself. I think he liked the *yes* more than the *me*. Real me fumbled with notebooks, and had difficulty completing sentences around him. I was the same way. I liked a golden boy who wanted me. I liked having a secret piece of him. I would close my eyes and think about it when I was by myself in bed at night, and feel a surge of something closer to power than to lust.

When we eventually tried to make it happen, at a house party in the second year of college, home for Christmas, I was extremely drunk. Drunk enough that without all those yesses in the past, it would have felt like he was taking what my dad called 'liberties'.

He made some comment about my pubic hair, that it got in the way. His was a thick forest that smelled of a long, hard day and some of it got caught in the back of my throat and I picked it out awkwardly in the taxi home.

Sex won't make people want you more if they don't really want you in the first place. I'd like to say that that was the end of Gary Shaw, but it wasn't. The night after the house party I took a shower and shaved off everything again. We messaged a bit awkwardly, but it wasn't as natural. The parameters of what we were had altered.

It felt strange, but I was used to feeling strange within my body. He hadn't used a condom and I worried about that to Maggie, while she congratulated me on my long game.

After that, there were a lot of boys. Some made me come, some didn't even try. But it was after that first time with Gary Shaw that I noticed the little pulse in the crease where hip met groin. At first it stung, like a large spot was developing, but the head never arrived. I had been shaving the edges and trimming around to keep my garden neat.

It stayed there, the lump, and after a time I sort of forgot about it. Every now and then, someone would ask me about it. I'd look at it, and say, 'Oh that. It's nothing to worry about. It's always been there'.

I felt that something permanent was less worrying than something new and strange. I didn't want to have an STD, but I was nervous about going to the doctor.

It kept on growing.

It was the size of a pea. And then a grape. In my more panicked moments I feared it was a testicle. I had read about babies that were born with both kinds of parts, and their parents arranged a quiet little snip. I was conscious of the thickness of my leg hair, the broad slope of my chest. Something had to happen or somebody would notice what I was. I started using tit tape to bind the lump to my leg. Then I made an appointment to see my GP.

She was an older woman, with tastefully greying hair. She wore a little brooch on her white coat. It had a small, round pearl on it, much like my grape had been before it grew to something else entirely.

I went with a cold. With doctors, they cost so much you want to save up three or four things. She told me I looked miserable.

I knew that she was right. My eyes had bags underneath them from lack of sleep and my fingers had broken out in little flaky stress bumps that I popped and peeled throughout the day and night. My stomach hurt. There were a lot of things wrong with my body. Inside and out. I found myself opening my mouth and telling her about the grape. My 'little growth'. She told me she would need a look at it, and turned her back while I removed my tights and knickers, got up on the examination table and felt the paper rough against my skin. She put on latex gloves, which smelled of powder. And she brushed her gloved fingers against the little border crease where leg met vulva. I spread my legs apart like I was on display, and when her eyes met mine I looked away. She prodded my grape with her finger.

'I see,' she said. 'It's a sebaceous cyst, I think. But just in case, I'll take a little swab. We might prescribe an antibiotic. And Cliona'll take your bloods before you go …'

I felt her trailing off, her fingers moving, squeezing. It felt less doctory, her face intent.

'I think,' she said again.

And something moved inside it at her touch. I felt it, and I think she felt it too, because her fingers stopped. She met my eye, and dropped her gaze again. Got the speculum and the long cotton bud and did her business. I sat there, opened up and closed off, answering questions about sexual partners.

'I have to ask,' she said.

I had to answer, lying there, legs spread, eyes fixed. I could still smell her gloves and something else, the meaty little tang of someone's body. I couldn't tell if it was hers or mine. I snorted mucus back into my throat and she told me that I was 'very chesty' and I nodded. I would listen to her. Take it easy. I would make sure to get some rest. Be careful.

She left me to my underwear and tights. To cover myself up. To go to Cliona, giving her three vials of my blood.

I was halfway to home when I felt it burst. I dashed inside a Starbucks, got the code and ran into the bathroom. The side elastic of my underwear was stained yellow-white, with a little blood, and there was something black or blue inside the grape. I prodded it, and tried to squeeze it out, like a blackhead. It was embedded, but I could feel it giving. And then there it was, small as the point of a needle: a little hair, nestled inside the grape. A seed inside the soft pulp of a berry. I pulled at it. It came. It kept on coming. I wound the blue-black fibre round my finger, and then around itself. It kept on coming out. Around, around. A little skein of thread that I had grown, and it was long and dark and it was gleaming coming out my body.

It was the strangest, most disgusting thing.

I wound it round my finger and I thought of Gary Shaw. Of Leon's face as mine crumpled beneath him. I thought of Maggie, the last time we spoke when she was back from Brighton for the Christmas. I thought of lying beside her when we were teenagers, the sweet tang of fizzy Haribo on her breath as she whispered in my ear and I felt special just the way I was. I thought of the small girl who showed her vulva to her mam. I thought of what it would be like to walk out of the cubicle and turn to the woman using the dryer, the woman washing her hands, the woman standing in her ballet pumps, and say:

'Look.

Look at this.

Look what my body did.

Isn't it awful.
Isn't it amazing.
I hate it and I love it.
And it's mine.'

But I am not a little girl now. I held the skein I'd made inside my hand, as small and soft as the baby mice that people feed their snakes. I put it in my pocket.

Stroked it with my thumb all the way home.

The Host

When we were small, we would visit my great-aunt Nóra's cottage in Spiddal, outside Galway. Nóra didn't live right beside the village, but when we sent her post-cards from our holidays in France the address said *Spiddal* above the *Galway, Ireland*. Nóra's house smelled like turf, and dough, and old warm rock. I would run my hand across the bumpy whitewashed walls and feel the shape of the stone beneath. The roof had once been thatched, but it was slated now. It looked odd, a box with the wrong lid.

I spent time there one Sunday in the month, sitting on the floor while my mother made conversation and my brother tried to sneak as many spoons of sugar into his tea as possible. We would eat bread. Or Rich Tea biscuits, smeared with proper butter. Spread so thick a yellow layer of it took on the irregular shape of encroaching teeth. She was a baker, and she was plain-spoken. My mother often said those things together. As though flour made you frank, something in the mixing, pouring, kneading.

I found out what rape was inside her house, an article I read in *Woman's Way*. I read another one about dolls that were possessed, and shoved all of mine right inside the wardrobe when we got home. You never know. Your doll can be a doll, but something happens, and all of a sudden you have to care for it, just like an infant. And it yells things at you, swears and bites and scratches. I would think of jagged plastic mouths upon my skin and shiver in the night.

Nóra was a houseproud woman and she kept a little garden round the back. That was for flowers; there were garden gnomes that stood around with little fishing poles beside the monkey puzzle tree. She didn't have a pond. I used to wonder. Ponds were very cool to me back then. They were what girls in fairy stories had. I loved to watch things that weren't human. I liked people, I did, but I was an awkward mix of precocious and strange. It didn't go down well with other children. I found myself reading more and more, and trying less. It was a strategy that served me well. My mother hated it. She liked me to be loudly, proudly clever, and didn't get why all the things she loved about me were resented.

I didn't want to be the best or brightest. I just wanted a friend.

Some years later, my parents were going through a rough patch in their marriage. They shouted a lot, at me and at each other. Sometimes they would try to keep it down, and I would listen to the low hum of hate in their voices and think of all the words I'd heard them spit and wonder what would happen. I didn't know that parents could split up. Before, I hadn't thought to worry, really. Things were the way that they had always been. I did not know that a family could shape-shift, like a witch into a hare when the thirst for milk was on her in the night. I had been told about shape-shifting women. They never scared me. Hares were only rabbits, or very like them. I had touched a rabbit on the back in Turoe Pet Farm. I knew that they were nervous and so soft.

'Prey animals are never fully calm,' the man in the polo shirt who took us round had said. I looked at shining berry eyes and recognized the panic. I worried that my touch had made things worse. I didn't want to hurt the little rabbit. But at the same time, I loved rubbing things.

My mother's patience was very short, because she was in pain. After my brother. I didn't know that then. I thought there was a badness in me. Something that the other children recognized as well. And I think back to that time, to being locked inside the hot press, nose pressed to the keyhole for the light. Counting to a hundred five times. Five more times again. My beating heart. I had a light beside me when I slept, but in the little room, the heat. The smell of warm, washed fabric. I think maybe because it was the daytime she didn't realize the dark was there. I do not think she had the space to think about it, really. When I had a nightmare, wet the bed, she would curl my little frightened body into hers, would stroke my hair. Would wash the sheets and put them back on the bed for the next night.

I come from kind people. Dinner in my mouth. Shoes on my feet. They loved me. They were trying. My parents ended up going off on a plane for several weeks to solve their problems. No one else was free, so Nóra took me.

Nóra was old then, but still sprightly. She kept the house clean and was famously good with money. My mother's sister was in hospital. My father's family lived overseas. But she was glad to take me. She'd tried to raise my mother, years ago. Back then my grandmother got very sick – they thought that she would die – and Nóra offered to take the baby. She couldn't have a child. This was back before her husband, my great-uncle Tom, got sick and died. Tom wore a flat cap and he was very tall. His skin looked soft and dry and when I felt his cheeks there wasn't stubble like my grandad had. Just all smooth. He wore a lot of brown and green and grey, and his voice was low and soft. They loved each other. When he went, she missed him. It was pneumonia, sneaking in behind some other things. I thought back then that it was just a cold, and when I got one I was fascinated. There was an importance to the fever-heat, the stuffed-up nose. As well as missing school, this thing could kill me. Even then, the thought attracted me.

We would sometimes be given old TK bottles full of water from Nóra's well, what my mother liked to call *fíor-uisce*, but I had never seen it. I liked the idea of a well. I pictured a storybook thing. A cylinder of stones and moss. A little wooden roof on top. A sprinkling of bluebirds, maybe squirrels.

The first night there, my mother dropped me off and I held her hand, like I was that bit younger than I was. The bed that Nóra gave me had a metal frame; it was from an old hospital she'd got it. It was very high, I had to climb. My mother gave Nóra the rubber sheet 'just in case'. My cheeks flushed red. I didn't like my body. It made me do things when I fell asleep. I felt betrayed.

Nóra grunted at me as I brushed my teeth. She didn't say much. Raidió na Gaeltachta was playing in the background. I understood some words. *Cogadh. Búama. Talamh. Gorta. Féar.*

That night I stayed awake for a very long time. I tried to play a game inside my head. The kind I made up when I needed to go somewhere else. It was about a crocodile.

Avoiding teeth. I counted near escapes like they were sheep, and watched my breath turn to fog. The night was cold, the range was off, the fire dying slowly. Flame by flame. The fog, it could be smoke. I'd be a dragon. But I was just a girl. Soft pink flesh.

The next morning, Nóra got up early. She didn't turn the television on, and instead of cereal there was bread and porridge. I ate it because I was a little scared of her. She cleaned out the ash and told me where to dump it. I complied. There were some thick dark hairs growing out of her chin. I looked at them, and rubbed my skin and wondered.

After breakfast we went to the well. It was a deep long crack inside the earth. I looked in and could feel the urge to topple. I waited for a warning that never came. Nóra was looking deep inside it too, holding a little bucket on a rope. It felt like it belonged in olden times. The stone the crack carved open was bleached grey, the mottle on it patchy with lichen.

'It's not a real well,' I said, disappointed.

She told me: 'It'll do.' We filled two large containers. Brought them back. The taste of it was something very different. There was a dusty tang, a note of something else. Almost sweet. I wasn't sure. I wondered what was down there.

Nóra had bought orange squash for me. She poured it onto a cup, filled it up with water. I said, 'Thank you.'

Manners were important.

Nóra worked all day long: she tidied, and she weeded, and she mended. The radio was playing. And I watched, and helped her when she told me. I'd brought ten books.

No dolls. Of course no dolls. I drank my squash and watched her and felt frightened. I wondered where my parents were, at all. And why, if they wanted to be a family, they would leave me. Surely I was the most important part of their familiness, a visible example. There would be no me without the two of them together. I didn't know what shape my life would take. I had friends with just a mother, none with just a father. They got new parents every now and then, step-people. I could feel the dread welling in me. I hated strangers. I read my books. I did my jobs for Nóra. Watched cartoons, if she left the house to go somewhere. I don't think a child the age I was would be left alone now, with the world the way it is. But there I was, and no predator came. Sometimes I would smell tobacco above the turf and I would think of Uncle Tom. It never occurred to me that Nóra would be sad.

Nóra ate the dinner at one o'clock in the day and it was always spuds. I had been trained to clear my plate but my stomach was unused to eating early. I had breakfast. Then lunch, a snack when home from school and dinner with my parents before bed. I ate her spuds, but I did not clear my plate and I could feel the hum of her contempt at the waste of it. I thought of her, going hungry as a child, the way my mother'd told me that she had in bedtime stories. And I really tried. I knew that I was lucky. I felt sad.

There was a tap in the side of Nóra's house. A brown tap that poked out of the wall. She would boil water for the tea, for the dinner, for the floor on the range in the kitchen or over the open fire in the sitting room. Whatever was free.

I remember the sound of water beating the bottom of the bucket and in my head it's mixed with the gush of the

boil, the beat of my heart. Something heavy and dangerous. Closing my eyes so tightly that the black turns almost
red. Thinking about the blood inside my eyelids, things
ebbing and flowing and making my body tick, grow
strong and sturdy. Sturdy was a word that people used
to describe me then. Sturdy body and a pretty face. I was
bigger than the other children in my class. And they knew
it and so did I. I don't remember when I first began to feel
a hulk, I do not know if it came all at once. Nóra liked the
size of me. She would call me a fine fat thing. Or a strong
little ox. I didn't like it and I didn't like the smell of flour
and tobacco that was on her. I would eat her soda bread
and sit beside her as she smoked and looked at the fire and
listened to the radio and I would wish I had another book,
another life and I'd be very tired.

I would go into the garden and pick out the weeds and
put them into a basket to be burned. I would dust the shelf
with all the little statues on it. Virgin Mary, Padre Pio. On
the wall there was a picture of Jesus and his mother. A red
light underneath it. Their chests were opened and their
hearts exposed, it was a miracle. Sometimes on my little
wooden stool I would reach my hand out to touch it. Nóra
hated that. She always knew. I didn't know how, but looking back it must have smeared the glass. Children's hands
are always slightly sticky. Even the clean ones have a sort
of patina. Only with goo not gleam. I hesitate to hold their
hands or touch their skin myself now. Everyone had told
me Nóra loved children. But she didn't. She would have
loved her own, I think. But she did not love me. I was a
favour she was doing for my mother who she loved. I was
an unformed hot thing ploughing through her tidy little
house. I would walk to mass with her. I would walk to the
shop and back again. My legs would get tired and I would

whine, but she would never listen. Eventually I stopped. There was no point. I counted my steps. The beat of my legs against the gravel road. I looked at the flowers in the hedgerow. The pink ones were my favourite. Clover, herb Robert, heather. The odd foxglove. Those were the best kind. I loved foxes and was very interested in anything having to do with them.

After a while, when Nóra walked with me to the well, my feet didn't hurt until the way back. I was getting stronger, used to labour. She made me hold the bucket and I was worried about what it would feel like when it filled up with water. That it would be heavy. That I would spill it and she would look at me like I was disappointing. She expected adult levels of competence from me. When she was growing up, children were little workers. You had them and they helped you on the farm. They didn't have the crusts cut off their toasts. A potato in their fists and out into the field with them. She stopped at the stony patch of earth.

The bucket lowered down. I lay on my stomach, looked deep into it. All I could see was darkness. The smell of wet stone. Moss. It still wasn't very impressive. There was no glamour to it. It wasn't the kind of well that princesses sat at, combing their long blonde hair and singing songs. I did not have long blonde hair, or a good singing voice, but I identified very strongly as a princess. I hated boys, but that was just because I hadn't met my prince yet. Clearly.

The water when it came was cold and heavy. My hands had a white line through the pink from the handle of the bucket when we returned. Nóra did not thank me for my help, I remembered. Though I had never thanked her for her hospitality. I was a child, I had always been cared for and considered it my due. In bed that night, I thought of

the deep crack in the rock, the ash inside the fireplace soft-
ening to grey from orange-bright. I felt like Snow White
here, tending to the cottage in the woods. I had carried
a bucket, I had swept the floor, dusted the vases and the
photographs. My legs and hands were tired. I missed my
parents. It had been too long. We were settling into our
own routine; I was becoming used to living in a version of
the past. My Irish was improving. I could understand more
of the radio now, the guttural rhythm of it. The 'nuchuda
nuchuda' my father had called it once, for what it sounded
like. It was turning into words. I did not know how.

The sheets were cold when I woke up, and I was shiver-
ing. I felt the creak of movement on the floor, but I was
curled inside the sheets and quilt.

'Nóra?' I asked, and my voice felt small and loud at the
same time.

There was no response.

Of course there wasn't.

I had known that it would not be Nóra. I closed my
eyes tight and felt my breath pierce my nostrils, lungs. Ice
in my throat, so cold it could have burned me, could have
numbed me. I felt something heavy and small clamber up
and sit upon my bed. I did not move. I stayed the way I
was. It stayed there for a long while, and when it left the
cold took time to lift. I woke up early and I left the room.
I sat on the small brown chair by the window, and stared
out at the garden, at the little ornaments, the coloured
petals of the different plants. Shop-bought ones – geraniums and busy Lizzies. I saw them and I did not look at
them. I stayed there, at the window for an age, until Nóra
was up and out and fed me.

I asked her when my parents would be back.

She said 'Soon', but did not give a timeline.

I wanted more but didn't care to ask. I sat and thought about the cold weight that had visited me. Was it Uncle Tom? But it was so small, the small thing on the bed. The cold of it.

It came again that night, and this time I could hear a low gurgling breath emerge from it, a sweet milky smell I did not recognize for what it was until much later on. It stayed where it was, and I stayed where I was. Eyes closed, breath held, until I fell asleep or it left. I would think of the water in the crack, the rush of it, the blood inside my body. It felt slower than it should have felt. The first time that I ever cut my leg I was both surprised and delighted. I hadn't realized that we could open up like envelopes, that there was so much to us. Blood excited me. It was so unexpected. Such a vivid shade under the pale.

The geraniums in Nóra's garden were red, and their petals looked a little softer than they were. I peeled them off and rolled them into little balls when she wasn't look-ing, and pulled off the buds from the fuchsia and popped them till the baby flower was open. It never looked right, but it was the sensation that drew me. The opening.

After several nights of little sleep, my skin began to smell not like my skin. It smelled of Nóra's house and something else. A mixture of the night-thing and the water I was drinking every day.

One night, the weight on my bed was wiggling slightly, little pointed shifts, and I felt worried that it would skitter up upon me like a spider. It did not. Its movements were more definite than that. For some reason I felt a different emotion course through my blood, a quickening this time. I was angry. This was my bed in Nóra's house. I kicked out my legs, trying to dislodge it, and my foot met fresh cold air. I did not know where I was. But it was not my room. I lifted up a corner of the sheet and saw the black of the country night. The stars like pinholes pricked into dark cloth. The moon like when the priest at mass broke the host in two. One of the bits. My family left mass straight after Communion, so I hadn't realized that there was more to it, until I stayed with Nóra. I hadn't made mine yet, and thought the people walking up and down looked silly, eating their little full-moon bits of bread.

The night was cold, but not as cold as the bed was. When I poked my toe out, it was a relief. I wanted to be away from the thing in the bed. I did not want to look at it. To see it. I felt that if I saw it, I would know it was there, and it would somehow be able to hurt me more. My eyes would make it realer, more tangible and threatening. I may have been confusing ghosts with bears. I was a child. I hadn't yet learned that, in certain circumstances, nothing helps.

I placed my foot on the grainy earth. I felt it pitted and almost warm against my feet. Like the skin of a lizard who has been lying in the sun, or the carapace of a turtle. Rough and bumpy. Firm. The stones felt decidedly alive that night, as though they were about to pulse, to beat. They did not do those things. I was not in fairyland, or a parallel universe or anything I had read about or seen in cartoons. I was in a place I knew. Beside the fissure deep inside the earth. Nóra's well. I remember telling myself to hold on to the bed, because I did not want to slip into the crack. I thought of the news. Of signs I had seen in town of people who got lost. Their flat smiling faces, fresh from the printer. Ink smudging in the rain. I felt something brush against my leg. It was about the size of a cat but it had skin instead of fur. Soft, cold skin. It moved clumsily. It smelled a little like my mother did when I snuggled into her neck at night, and of something else as well. A bit like me, perhaps. I startled, then. I could not help myself.

Later she said that I had fallen in, but at the time, I remember thinking I was being swallowed. Large rocky pebble teeth, a limestone tongue, wet and porous. I can recall the fall but not the landing. I must have landed in the water, because I was wet through when she found me the following morning. I was lying on my back, beside the crack. My fingertips were raw and I had large black rings around my eyes. Nóra looked at me like I was a child and not a stranger.

'Come here to me, *a leana*,' she said, and gathered me up in her arms and carried me to the house. She was old but very strong; I could feel her muscles against my legs. I was crying and I worried that I was making too much noise. That tears and snot would stain her blouse and make her impatient with me. But it didn't. When we were back indoors, she made me a cup of tea with three spoons of sugar in it and asked me to tell her what happened.

I didn't know how to put it into words.

'Did it visit you?' she asked at last. 'The little one?'

I nodded and sipped the sweet, hot tea. It burned the roof of my mouth and I could taste the little grains of sugar adhering to it.

'It was cold in the bed,' I told her.

'It is, at that,' she replied. 'Did you fall in the well?'

'I remember falling, but …'

'Not the getting out?'

I nodded. I felt the tears well up in my eyes again. I had cried on the way home and again when she had brought me the tea. I wanted my mother and I felt very confused by what had happened. Even looking back on it now, I remember the sensations as though they happened to another child. I know that child is me, but another version. Another separate self.

'What will happen now?' I asked.

She looked at me for a long time, and pulled herself up from her chair to sit on the arm of mine.

'When I was a child, like you are now, I was in the well for a time too. They found me, like I found you, beside it, wet and there was a terrible scare on me. I wouldn't tell them and I couldn't tell them what had happened. I put it from my head. I married Tom. But when I fell asleep, I knew there was a cold thing in my room. The cold small thing you saw. It was what the well took from me. There's a hunger in that water. It doesn't hurt you as you are now. But it takes something small from what you could be. Love or health or money. Some small important thing. It took my baby from me. I didn't know until I wanted it and then I knew. I kept on trying, wanting. But there wasn't a point to it. The well had swallowed up the future where I got to have a child.'

I looked at her.

'I don't know what it will take from you,' she told me. 'But you will have a visitor, and soon. And there will come a day when you know what that visitor is or could have been.'

And I did. And there was.

Nóra died, and left the cottage to a distant cousin who wouldn't live there. The slates grew moss and the walls flaked like dry skin. The garden grew to wilderness, the gnomes covered by the green, the flowers choked by different types of weed. There were some foxgloves. I took you there the day after it happened. We had visited my uncle who lived nearby. And I had felt the soft brush of the presence against my shoulder, cheek. Like a lover's touch. It was a gentle thing, what haunted me.

I showed you the garden, and the little door. The lace curtains disguised the inside, but I described the peach and brown walls, the Sacred Heart. It sounded, you told me, like your grandfather's house in County Leitrim. I smiled at you. We went around the side and pulled the little blue gate, looked at the tap on the outside of the wall, turned it and watched it spit brown drops.

'It would be a lovely place to do up,' you said. 'If you had money, you could really make a home here.'

I thought of Nóra's hands kneading bread. Slapping dough on flour, the yellowing skin and the thick veins. How hard she worked. You never know how long the fall will be. Until you reach the bottom. My parents stayed together for a time, until they didn't. It changed a lot for me, and very little. I was well taken care of. I never told them about the well. I had no words to share the strange, dark thing. An adult thing, to happen to a child.

You took a cutting of a rose bush in bloom. You tried to grow it, but of course it died.

There was a sweep through the garden, and you gripped my elbow, turned me back to look. Something was moving slowly through the grass. It could have been a fox, a neighbour's cat. You love animals and tried to stay and watch it. But the wind was cold and I walked back to the car. I waited for you to join me and I thought of the awkward sweep of bush. The soft, cold skin. What even is a memory, in fairness? A little tale, a dead thing living on. You hopped in beside me, and I started the ignition before you'd even clicked the seat belt in. We drove back

138

past my uncle's, and past the ocean, out the road towards the motorway.

And every tree that moved a little hand.

Her Face

The drive home from the office is second nature. Eve could do it blindfolded, if it weren't for pedestrians and traffic lights. It's the closest thing to quiet time she gets. She takes a big, deep breath, and turns the key. The car is getting old, she'll change it sometime, when they can afford it. She scrolls through cars sometimes, in bed at night – something reliable, and maybe diesel this time to save money. In the long run. The car is cold at first, this spring is sharp. It took a while for winter to get going, and it's taking longer still for it to ease. She has her coat, her hat, her little scarf, but still she needs the welcome blast of heat. Her skin feels itchy, tight. It seems to shrink on her throughout the day. She has a big round patch of eczema, the size and shape of a two-euro coin, inside her elbow at the bend of skin. She rubs cream into that every single night, but the only thing that helps is time.

She gets it every year.

It really bugs her.

Her phone is almost out of battery so she sticks the radio on. The news is grim. It always is. People with more energy than her protest unfairness. Her mother says 'those people have no jobs' when she sees protesters in town. But that's not it. When something matters, people make the time, Eve thinks. But how do you begin to know what matters when there's so much constantly going on? And the same things crop up over, and over again, in the end, it doesn't make a difference. People say things, but they don't get heard. The patch returns, each winter. Nothing changes.

She turns the rear-view mirror to avoid the little scrape of face reflected in it. She knows just how she looks. The mirror doesn't have to rub it in. By the end of the day, her foundation caked in places, smooth in others. Mascara on the underside of eyes. She keeps some baby wipes under her seat. For bird shit, not for babies. And if it gets really bad, she could reach down, and pull one out and scour the whole thing off.

Some people can do makeup properly, not daub it on. The more she tries, the more she seems to fail. At the red light she reaches into the pocket of the door for hand cream and rubs it on her dry patch, on her hands. The other driver beeps when it goes green, and she startles, twists her head to the rear-view mirror to see who beeped, who was annoyed by the small delay of her trying to help herself a little bit. She read a thing online about finding times within the day for self-care. But she's so busy when she gets back home. Niall picks up the kids, and that's a good thing, but there's dinner to be made, lunches to sort for the next day, and she'll need to find out how they are, give them baths and wash their clothes. Emily's coat is always getting dirty. And she only has one coat that she likes to wear, so it's hard to even give the coat a day off to dry.

The other driver's face is grim, familiar. The line of mouth. The hair. It could well be her mother. The jolt of that. The fear. The car turns off. Eve wondered if it was her. And did she know who Eve was, when she beeped. She is the kind who would just beep anyway. Who would express annoyance loudly, easily. It was other people's she couldn't take.

It has been thirteen months since they last saw each other.

She calls sometimes. Or texts.

Eve won't reply.

She rubs her eyes again and the mascara gets into them and suddenly they're stinging and it isn't tears. It isn't fucking tears but the timing is annoying and if she gets home and Niall sees her eyes red and she tells him that she saw her mother he will make a thing of it and it isn't one. It doesn't matter anymore. It doesn't. She pulls a Kleenex from her bag, and another driver beeps at her, but this time it's because the car was drifting. Jesus, that was dangerous. She could have killed someone, could have been hurt. And Emily. And Eoin. They're too small to be without their mother.

What if they grow up and she does something and they start to hate her? To push themselves away. What if she hurts them in ways they can't explain and so it comes out as aggression all the time, in every conversation? What if she starts to pick at them, bit by bit? When they stretch out and learn how to be inside the world. Find plans to make that might not be the ones she would have chosen.

It's a lot.

Eve turns down their road, and her phone whirrs with a message from Niall.

We need milk and toilet roll.

She nods. Even though there's no one there to nod to.

She looks up.

A different car, but is it that same face again inside it?

It's a green Toyota Yaris.

It's not her mother.

Brain just playing tricks.

Her mother wouldn't drive that sort of thing.

Eve needs to stop it.

The other make of car, the red Golf.

That's the one she has now.

Even though Eve didn't spot the reg.

And she would know.

If they had changed the car.

Someone would have said.

That mouth.

That hair.

She'll swing by Lidl. Pick up the few bits. They need other things too: apples, and frozen peas and tins of beans and pasta and vegetable oil and probably those small packets of raisins. And jam. Emily loves jam. She wants jam on everything.

She'd put jam on a steak, Niall said once, and Eve said she would too, and they smiled at each other and the love they had for Emily kind of made a blanket around them and it was nice. That's one of her favourite things about Niall. What a good dad he is. And how it feels to love the kids together. Watch them grow.

Eve's mum had called Emily a greedy child. Greedy like her mother. A little savage.

Eve didn't like that but she let it slide. She didn't have the words to tell her mother exactly why the way she was was wrong, and there would be no point. If she made a thing of it, her mother would start telling every visitor she had that Emily had no manners on her, and that she was addicted to sugar, and probably going to end up diabetic.

144

Or worse. It was easier to take that sort of thing when it was only about Eve herself. And Emily is fine. There's nothing wrong with jam. Jam is not the worst thing you can give to a child.

Eve indicates into the car park, and reverses into a small space. The car beside her has parked a bit over the white line, so she slides over the gearstick and gets out of the passenger seat instead. She thinks of the people who couldn't do that, like Niall who is too big, and her father who has mobility issues after that thing with his legs and back. It takes ten seconds to tidy up the car if you get it wrong the first time, like. It's just respect.

Eve hardly speaks to her father anymore either. It's hard to organize a time to meet. For him to see his grand-children. She's worried that he'd be reporting back all the time to her mother and it sours things and she feels guilty because she's the one who soured them. She's the one who chose to walk away. He makes it difficult as well, because he'll always take her mother's side when it comes down to it. Even when she's wrong, she's never wrong.

Eve takes a basket, not a trolley, but she fills it up and has to carry the toilet roll under her armpit, and it's awkward.

She buys three things of jam. The jars are nice, she can use them for something after. Lentils or what have you. Eve likes a decent jar. They had them on the tables at the wedding. With tea lights and lacy strands that matched her dress. That was before the kids though, and now if they break it's dire. Lots of cleaning up and organizing it so small soft feet don't get shards of glass in them. It was easier when they were little babies. You plonked them down somewhere and there they were. Which must be hard enough on them, in fairness. No wonder they learn to crawl, or bum-shuffle in the case of Eoin, who motors around the place on his arse with frankly incredible speed.

At the wedding, her father spoke, and said such lovely things about Eve and Niall. Wishing them every happiness. Eve's mother was on her best behaviour that day too. She looked great in her cream dress and bolero, and they weren't by themselves for long enough for her to start pointing out inadequacies. Though they were noted, she saved them up until they were back from the honeymoon. The soup. The centrepieces. The tables looked like a recycling bin. It didn't bother Eve that much, in fairness. She was good at shrugging some things off.

The shopping comes to €23.98 and she pays by card. She tells the woman thank you. When she gets back to the car the green Yaris is parked beside her. She looks inside it, for clues. There's very little. It's clean, but there are some little twigs on the floor, like someone went for a walk and took half the forest home with them. In the back seat there might be dog hairs. Eve's mother can't bear dogs. But sometimes she goes walking with her friend Ann who has a bichon frise who's very good and she makes an exception for him. Sparkle. Ann's daughter, Laura, named him. Sparkle must be pushing twenty now. How long do dogs live? He could well be dead. Eve wouldn't know.

'Are you all right?' asks someone and Eve almost jumps out of her skin. It's a man, tall and broad, with glasses. He is wearing a check shirt, like Niall sometimes. Like every man sometimes. His voice isn't angry, just a bit confused. Eve tells him she's fine, and unlocks her own car and gets in. She hates being caught out being weird in public. And it is weird – peeping into someone else's vehicle. But there's no law against it. It isn't call-the-guards type weird. Eve peers over at the car. She was definitely seeing things. That man looked nothing like her mother. It would be nice to know, wouldn't it though. Who people are. If there was an app on your phone you could download and point at the car and it could just say:

Moira, 63, Glentubber Heights

or

Jim and Ashley Nowak, mid-twenties, Riverside Grove

or

Not Your Mother, Eve

Eve used to be on her phone more, she was a great one for the Instagram, particularly when Emily was small. She had more time. But then after they fell out, her mother shared one of the pictures she'd posted to Facebook, with a comment that pretended she'd been in the room as well. And Eve rang her to ask her to take it down and she'd refused and said she was 'entitled' to her grandkids.

Eve told her that no one was entitled to anyone. And that she was sick of her making things more difficult than they needed to be. And her mother said she wouldn't be long changing her tune when she was dead and gone. And Eve said that anyone could die. Just because she was old didn't mean that she was any closer to it than another person. Brian Power, a boy down the road, had dropped down dead the day before his twenty-first birthday and sure the doctors still didn't know what happened there.

And her mother said that she was being selfish, that she was always out for herself first, and that she couldn't believe a creature like Eve had come out of her, and that her father was so ashamed of her, and wearing a path to mass to light candles that she'd not be such a bitch.

And Eve told her that he was in his hole doing that, not with his back, and that she was sick, sick of her. And she'd hung up the phone and cried tears that were so hot that her eyes felt swollen and infected with them and she'd hated that she was crying, and that she couldn't change the way she was or the way her mother was or how they were together. And she'd made herself a cup of tea and as the kettle boiled, she blocked her mother on all her social media accounts. And then Eoin had woken up and cried as well and she hadn't even time to drink the tea. Niall had taken Emily off to Smyths that day, because she'd been so good at doing her wees in the toilet all week, and by the time they came home, Eve was calmer, feeding Eoin in the big soft rocking chair that had been a present from Niall's parents who were so good and always offering to take the kids if they ever wanted a night out or a weekend away. Eoin's little eyes were clouded over with the joy of nourishment, and Eve was looking up counsellors on the phone.

She'd never even gone to one after that. She was afraid that somehow her mother would find out. Or that it would be like admitting that she was mentally unhinged and therefore in the wrong on all accounts. Eve's friend Sadhbh went to a counsellor when they were teenagers and she'd had that thing with food. John from work had seen someone for a while, after his husband died. But that was different. Compared to them, Eve was lucky. Grand. Better to just completely cut off contact for a while. She didn't think then that it would stretch so long. But every time her mother contacted her, Eve felt annoyed and hurt. And the days she didn't hear from her were a relief.

Seasons changed, and still the ache of it remained. And somehow, Eve made a ghost of her. She felt her every day, in some small way. Sometimes she would be coaxing Emily to eat her vegetables, or giving them their bath and she would remember all of the good things her mother had done too. And she would feel so sad that it had come to this, and wonder what would happen if one day she woke up and stopped liking her kids. Started seeing them with different eyes. It wouldn't happen. The two of them were very different people. Today was just a bad day. She was being irrational. Just because her mother was exactly the type of woman who would have Eve followed, who would recruit family and neighbours to report back, who had in fact done both of those things over the past thirteen months, didn't mean that Eve wasn't safe today.

Seat belt on.

Too tight.

She must redo it.

Eve reverses out and almost hits a child. A small brown-haired boy, with thick glasses kept on with elastic. He lets out a squawk and runs towards his mother. Thankfully, she was putting bags into the car and didn't notice. Eve's heart thumps so hard against her chest. She knows that she should get out, check on him. Apologize. But she can't take one thing, one more little thing today. She'll lose it. He doesn't need a stranger crying at him. He needs his mam to give him a big hug.

He will be fine. But children are so fragile, so much about them that the world can break. They have more bones than adults do, for one thing. And babies have that soft spot on their head, the fontanelle. It doesn't close up rightly, not for ages after they're born. Before Emily, Eve thought they just had one, but there are four of them. So the skull can shift, on the way out, adapt to the small space it finds itself in. Eve remembers running her fingers over Emily's head, the crisp of cradle cap, the velvet hair, and the feeling of something fathomless inside.

And what would it be like, to hurt a child. To want to hurt your own child, over and over. To chip away at her, shard by shard. Nobody can hurt you like your mother, Sadhbh said once, and there is such a bang of truth to that, it frightens Eve. When Emily gets jam all over her coat that's just been cleaned she feels herself getting frustrated, primed to snap, she wonders if this will be the time that something starts to crack that will not heal. There are things Eve's mother has done to her that Eve cannot forget. Her mother doesn't even remember half of them, and will deny them flat out, or shrug and say 'well if you say so', or 'did I do nothing right at all at all?' or 'you were always that way, holding grudges'.

Emily's little face looks so like Niall's sometimes. But her expression when she's hurt is Eve, all Eve, and Eve is scared of that. Of all that binds them, and how easily those bonds can break apart. And she tries not to, she really, really does, but she finds these mean thoughts crowding in her sometimes. Resentments, and she knows it's natural, all mothers feel frustrated now and then, but what if one day, she kills something and doesn't know it's dead until much later?

She meets her own eyes in the mirror, and they hate her and she knows they hate her.

She has her mother's face. Foundation in the cracks around her mouth, the inside of her elbow thirsty, aching.

It doesn't stop.

It never fucking stops.

And home she goes.

I Want to Know That I Will Be Okay

When we were children, we used to climb over the limestone wall at the end of the garden, and walk through the
overgrown fields our grandfather had farmed, towards
that house. Our legs would feel the tickle of the grass and
sometimes the sting of it, from the hard sharp blades that
left small red marks, a bit like paper cuts, if they got you
right. Sometimes ticks or sciortáns would cling to our legs
but we never noticed them till later on when, hot in bed,
we'd kick the sheets and rub and pick at our legs for something to do when it was early still and sleep was as hard to
catch as our cousin Nadia, who was the fastest one of us.
She would lose us in the fields, would leave us there if we
could not keep up. We'd watch her back moving further
and further away and disappearing. When we got older, I
would see that back moving through crowds in bars and
at house parties. We would arrive together and then we'd
separate, and she would melt in easily and remind me, but
that when she had the choice, she would choose to spend
her time with other, better people.

I was a child who liked to read, who liked to pick at
things. I hated the outdoors but when we were together,
I wasn't the one who got to make the choices. We played
forty-forty, or tag, or games of Nadia or Cian's invention

with names like Lightning Strike or Avalanche. Sometimes I wondered if the games were designed to keep me apart from them, to make me hide or chase while they escaped, laughing. Thinking now, I'm fairly sure they were. They loved to lose me.

Once I found a sciortán, plump and burrowed into the soft skin at the back of my knee. It took a nail scissors to get it out and when my mother woke me the next morning, she didn't notice the blood on the sheets. Even when they went in the wash she didn't spot it and the stain baked in. It mustn't have been as dramatic as the quasi-surgical operation I remember, where I gritted my teeth like a wounded soldier taking out bullets. I couldn't get a proper look at the sciortán, as I worked on it, it broke apart, but what parts I could find were black. It left a little hole behind my knee, like a big pore that I could stretch the skin of and fit the whole tip of my smallest finger inside. I didn't show it to anyone, but I would sometimes do it, to remind myself that I could. It made me feel the way I felt when adults did disturbing things to scare me, like my Mamó poking out her false teeth and pulling them back in with her darkly purple tongue. She could move them like mandibles. Clicking and alien. It made me cry, but Cian would scream at her: *Again, again.*

I was a quiet child, pale and pretty. People would remark on my face. My large eyes, especially. Mam dressed me in little patterned dresses and ankle socks. I was well into school before I realized that I could ask her for different clothes. I thought that you just had what was in the wardrobe, and sometimes a new thing appeared, and you wore it when you were told to and took it off at night and it might go away for a while if it was dirty but it always came back, until I got too big for it. I didn't touch the world very much back then. It kind of rolled and pulsed around me, pushing me one way or another, but never very far or very hard.

I didn't grow up pretty. But by then, I'd learned to be glad of that. I didn't like people looking at me. It was never the right pair of eyes, or the right look. There was always something wrong. When we got the renovations done, they put a new window into the bathroom and one of the builders took me in there and showed me the small, two-brick space they'd cut to begin the window. He leaned in to my ear and said, *Will we just leave it that way, princess?*, and I roared crying, and Mam apologized to him for me. What a fright I'd given that poor man. I heard about it until I was well-grown. It was one of the stories we told about each other, like Cian getting ten out of ten in his spellings five weeks in a row and the teacher telling the whole class they didn't have any homework because of how great Cian was. Or me trying to jump after him onto a small round patch in the centre of a stream in Barna Woods, and wetting my tracksuit that Auntie Nuala had sent me from Australia, and spoiling the day on all of them. Mam had goaded me to try, with the jump. I knew that I wasn't good enough to make it. My legs didn't work as quickly as my brain did and so I always trailed a bit behind.

I wasn't a complete waste of space. I liked to sing, and Mam encouraged that, so I thought I was good at it until the teacher asked me to just move my mouth at our Communion mass and let the other children make the sounds. Mam was raging with her. She liked my voice. I liked it too. Especially when there was no one there to hear it, and I could make all kinds of strange noises in my throat and with my cheeks and not worry about being weird but just take that part of me for a little adventure. I was great at adventures when I was by myself. It was when I tried to get other people involved that playing got difficult. They never understood what was interesting about my games, and I didn't have the words to make them see it. I wasn't fun. I was intense and very bossy for a quiet child.

Daideo's was what we called the big abandoned house behind Nadia's house, the one where she and Auntie Margaret lived. It had been Mamó's father's house and when he died it had been left to rot, because if Uncle Fiachra sold it he'd have to split the money with Mam and Auntie Margaret, and he didn't fancy doing that at all. Tight as a tick, Mam called him, and I thought of the little sciortán, burrowing its way inside of me and filling up with some of what I was. Sometimes Auntie Margaret would go off for a while and Nadia would live with us and we were never told why exactly, but we accepted it.

Auntie Margaret's house was a twenty-minute walk from ours if you went through the fields, and it had been built from a catalogue by our grandfather to encourage his eldest son to stay at home, but Uncle Seán went off instead to America and met a man over there that had been a priest and wasn't now. They lived together and I don't know if they were happy or not because they never came back here for us to check. The old abandoned house smelled of wet wallpaper and dry powder. Cian told me that teenagers went drinking there, and smoking, as if those were the two worst things that people could do, and I knew even then that he wouldn't be long taking up both of them when he got the chance.

Nadia had been in there a few times, but Auntie Margaret told her it was dangerous, and to stay away from it. It didn't look dangerous. It looked sad. Nadia told us that we weren't allowed there because something lived inside it. She said there was an old woman who had lived there before Great-Grandad Padraig and she had a daughter and the daughter had a child and the woman killed the child to save the daughter from the shame of it. I asked Nadia why, and she rolled her eyes and told me that some people didn't like it when women had babies by themselves with no dad there. I wanted to ask more things but she shushed me.

The old woman waited for the little one to creep out into the world, Nadia said, and held her breath steady and her knife sharp. And when it came out she cut off its head and buried it under the stairs, but the daughter wanted her baby and her heart broke and she went mad and had to go to a place for women whose brains didn't work anymore and her mother told everyone that she had killed her own baby and was unnatural, but that was just a lie.

When the daughter was gone, the old woman had no one to talk to and no one around the house. And so she started talking to the ghost of the baby. And when she gave her words and attention to it, she gave it power. It ate up everything she said and wanted more, like a hungry mouth sucking on the rubber at the top of a bottle. Filling its cheeks. And slowly it remembered the hand that had held the knife, and the bright world going dark and the sorrow in the space where its mother was supposed to be. And it decided that the old woman needed to pay. And so, one night, it began to cry. The woman woke up frightened by the sound, and went to walk down to the back kitchen where all of this had happened and where the noise was coming from. But ghosts, even small ghosts, can be in more than one place at once, and though this was the ghost of a baby, the beginning and the end of life having been so close together made it strong.

And it crawled under her foot at the top of the stairs and she fell down to the bottom, but she wasn't dead, so it shuffled down on its stomach and crept like a cat onto the top of her chest, and it put its hungry baby-mouth on her mouth and sucked the breath from out of her lungs and swallowed it up until its little ghost belly was round and fat with nourishment.

Our great-grandad had gotten the house cheap because of what had happened with that woman, but no one wanted to live there in the end, because if you thought about the baby or told anyone about it, the baby would wake up and remember how hungry it was, and begin tormenting you. Nadia warned me never to tell the story to anyone, and I never did, though later on I wondered if she might have made it up. It was the kind of thing she liked to do. To scare me and to look at my face being scared and to smile.

I didn't often go near that house after that if I could help it, even when we grew into teenagers. Nadia always knew what to say and where, and I hung off of her whenever we were together, which was mainly outside of school because she was in a different year and had her own friends who didn't like me much. Mam didn't know what to make of me, as my prettiness faded and my awkwardness remained. I held on to some of the mannerisms of a cute child and would do things that made her embarrassed for me sometimes, like kiss her on the cheek when she dropped me at the school, and ask her to tuck me in. I could feel how far apart I was from adulthood, and how bad I would be at it and so I clung to the things that had worked for me before, but could feel them no longer working, and wondered why everything was going wrong.

I thought long and hard about everything that came out of my mouth and it was never the right thing anyway. Cian was better at people, because he didn't care about them so much. He went to the boys' school and I was in the girls' school and it was for the best because I didn't want him to know how hard it was for me, though it was obvious. I wrote in my diary at night, and lied to it, telling it I had friends I didn't have and that I was involved in all of the drama I slowly picked up through Nadia, or by sitting beside people who talked to each other. I didn't want to commit a life I wasn't happy with to paper. Paper deserved more than what I was.

I made a friend called Sylvia halfway through the year. She was a little wispy thing, and would sometimes drift off while you were talking to her, as though she'd seen a butterfly she knew and had to keep track of where it was off to. She came to my house and I went to hers, and we'd message each other in the evenings. She had been friends with a girl called Suzanne earlier in the year, but Suzanne was friends with other people now, and had called her weird and clingy and sent horrible messages about her behind her back. A girl called Lauren had shown them to her, and Sylvia had had to leave Science class because she was crying so much that snot went on her notebook and everyone saw.

It was nice to have a friend, and we would go to town together on the weekends and look around the shops. There were some bands and books that we both liked and we would talk about those, and if she looked bored I would bring up Suzanne so she could bitch about her. I'd learned from Nadia that people liked to bitch about their enemies, and rarely got tired of it. There was a girl called Stacey that Nadia had given a black eye to once and almost gotten suspended, even though Stacey had started the whole thing. Nadia had grown fearsome and liked to fight her friends. She had tried to fight me a few times, but I didn't give her much satisfaction because there wasn't much fight in me. I didn't want to hurt her or get hurt. Nadia was always talking about getting Stacey back and what she was going to do to her. She never got specific about it, though. Cian didn't really hate anyone, though he thought he was better than everyone else. Mam agreed with him, and got him the best of everything. He was given a fiver every day to buy his lunch, while I had to prepare my own sandwiches, to teach me independence and hard work. Cian did rowing and he needed to have everything the other boys had, from clothes to money.

Dad was working in the States a lot back then. He came back later, when he lost his job. Dad was a side character in our lives, and Mam was worried about Cian not having any male role models, and was glad he was so involved in rowing. She kept telling me it was good for a lad to hang out with a pack of other lads. She used the term *pack*, like they were wolves. She didn't like Sylvia, and called her sly sometimes. I wondered if she was being racist, but she told me not to be silly, that anyone could be sly, no matter what colour their skin was, and that it was foolish of me to rely so much on one friend. I didn't want to explain to her that I couldn't get another friend, that I didn't have the thing it took to make a person fun, and that I knew Sylvia would be bored with me soon, and that if we fought, she wouldn't miss me the way she missed Suzanne. No one could feel that kind of rage about me, unless I was their disappointing child.

Mam would sometimes scream at me, for someone to scream at. Dad was too far away, and Cian too loved. I hoovered lazily, and missed the corners of rooms. I stained my knickers when I had my period and put them in the wash without scrubbing them first. It wasn't her job to scrub them, and I knew that. But I didn't want Cian to see, and smirk at me the way he always did. It seemed shameful enough to be as awkward a thing as I was in comparison to him. I didn't even like going to the bathroom when I had my period and would wait and wait in class to avoid raising my hand, and then regret it when I saw the stains left on the soft flesh of my inner thighs from the blood beading out of the wings like dew on leaves.

I was surprised when Nadia and Cian invited me to the party they were having at Daideo's house, but I suppose they had to. We had always been the three of us. I was excited and hungry for more of life. I had read about people who were happy in books and they always seemed to be doing things, but when I did things I still felt like I was waiting for Mam to pick me up from school, and she was running late, standing and staring and trying to do something with my body to hide my distress, my feeling of being increasingly unloved and exposed.

They wanted to have *a thing* in the old house while Auntie Margaret was away for the weekend. We didn't have to worry about Mam, who slept like a log. She was taking pills to help her with that, and they knocked her out completely. It seemed to take her longer and longer to be herself in the morning, and she'd drink her coffee, and gesture to our schoolbags with the look of a woman who was half-in, half-out of her own skin. I expected to see it pooling on the floor sometimes like a duvet that had been wrapped around her. Her head grew straighter on her neck bit by bit and by the time she dropped us to school she looked exactly like a person looks, and could pay attention to whatever little thing we wanted to say. When she'd been insomniac, it hadn't been better, but it had been more familiar. She had been like two hands, pulling taut at a cat's cradle until it dug into the skin hard enough to leave a mark. If I woke to go to the bathroom, she would be sitting at the kitchen table, back erect, drinking camomile tea, because it was supposed to relax her and the doctor had told her she wasn't allowed to have caffeine after seven p.m. She went through months of this until he relented and gave her the sleeping tablets. I was happy she could sleep, but she didn't seem any better, to be honest. Just a different kind of strange. I took one once, to see what it would do to me, and I just sat there, waiting for something to happen, until I realized that it wasn't going to.

The party, though of course they were too cool to call it a party, needed a bit of planning, and we spent time in the old house, hauling planks of wood out to make space, and covering rotten floorboards with bits of plywood we found in the shed. Nadia stole all of Auntie Margaret's candles, and the fairy lights that you put batteries into. Cian got camping lamps from his friends, and scattered them around the building. It felt a bit like we were kids again, building a clubhouse. I gathered sleeping bags and blankets and tied them up in bin bags so they wouldn't get wet or nibbled on by rats. Nadia asked me not to invite Sylvia, and it hadn't occurred to me that I would. It was so fully their world and they had always been able for things I wasn't. When they talked about the future, they just assumed they would meet someone, have a family. I never took any of that for granted. Loneliness seemed inevitable, and I knew I would have to hustle to avoid it.

The night of the party, I just wanted to go to bed and stay there. Nadia was to meet us at Daideo's. Cian showered and was basically ready, but I had to worry about what people wore when they hung out in groups. I went for jeans and a nice t-shirt, like what Nadia wore when she went to town. We went to bed as normal and waited until half past eleven and then I heard Cian sneak out and I got up and followed him. I was wearing mascara and tinted moisturizer and a bit of bronzer on my cheeks. My hair had been straightened and re-curled, and then messed a little so it didn't look too obviously nice. I brought a big sweatshirt and a fleece because I knew it would be cold, and looked at Cian striding on ahead and wondered if he would have woken me up at all, if I hadn't heard him. It had been Nadia who had talked to me the most about what was going on.

When I arrived in the house, there were about twelve other people there, some of Cian's friends from rowing, and Nadia had invited Lauren, and some other girls she knew. They had naggins and bottles in brown paper bags and cans and I didn't know what to drink, I hadn't thought to bring anything. Nadia gave me a bottle of 7UP that tasted like there was nail polish remover in it, and I sipped on it and tried to look like I wanted to be there, and like I would be a good person to talk to, or to kiss. I felt like everyone my age had kissed someone, and I was the only one who hadn't, but I couldn't imagine the steps from talking to kissing. Romance novels were no help because the people in them seemed to love each other in a range of impractical ways, quirkily or fiercely. Nadia didn't seem to care about the boys she'd been with. She'd mention it in passing and roll her eyes if I asked follow-up questions, saying things like, *That's just Fitzy though* or *like I give a fuck*.

I drank what was in the bottle Nadia had given me, and I must have seemed all right because she gave me more. Margaret, I knew, kept vodka in because my mam had said so. Mam didn't, but she did have a bottle of brandy that she kept in the little press above the wardrobe where we hung our coats. Cian had, apparently, given money to his pal Seán who could buy drink for him. I looked at my hands and put them on my knees and then put my palms together like I was praying and then dropped them down by my side. I thought of that ghost baby Nadia had talked about, crawling and weaving its way under and around everyone's legs, and being very old and very young at once. I rubbed my eyes and when I stopped rubbing them there was mascara on my hands. I went outside and sat on a pile of firewood and tried to use my phone to see what the damage was but it was too dark and I couldn't use my camera and my torch at the same time. I heard someone say: *Cian's sister's out there pure crying*, and a laugh. And I felt so ashamed of who I was and so powerless to be anything else and I didn't want to go home because they would make fun of me for leaving. So I went back into Daideo's and up the old rotting stairs, carefully and quietly, and into the small room above where everyone was gathered. I could hear the birds up in the rafters getting irritated that somebody was there. I put my two hands on the floor and felt the dust and bird shit underneath them and I lay there, listening and looking through a small hole in the floorboards. I couldn't see very much. It was dark.

I thought that no one knew where I was but after about an hour Cian came up and asked me what the fuck I thought I was doing, and said that I was weird and he was mortified by how weird I was, and my fucking face, and I stood up and brushed myself down, and I knew that everyone could hear him saying these things to me, and it was quieter now, and I felt that they were true, that all the things I feared about myself were no longer something I could just explain away as my own anxiety. I wanted someone to tell him to leave me alone, but no one did and once I stood up I realized that I was drunk now. I hadn't been drunk before but I knew that I was because I was definitely going to vomit. And I did, and it slithered through the floor, and I heard someone make a loud disgusted noise and then laughter and talk returned. And everything was patchy after that, but I remember Nadia holding me, her hands on my bare arms and telling me I needed to be quiet, and my own shrill voice, piercing through it all over and over. I want to know that I will be okay. I want to know that I will be okay. And no one telling me that I would be, or could be. Because how could they? Look at what I was.

And suddenly everyone was gone, and I was lying down and it was quiet. My face was on the floor and something was very gently rubbing my back, not in the way that a human hand would, but like a cat kneading with their paws. Up and down, a small insistent march. And I tilted my head and looked through the small hole again, and the vomit must have been cleaned up or something because it wasn't there. It smelled different too, like the Palmer's body butter Sylvia used, and the small bottle of tea rose perfume I'd gotten from The Body Shop with my Christmas voucher, coffee grounds and wet wool and fresh bread. And I felt, then, that this was the place for me, and the motions on my back maintained their pace. And through the hole I could see a different sort of space, one that didn't fit the shape of the room. It wasn't what I expected to see, but there it was and I couldn't look away, the small paws moving, I was not afraid. There were two people in the room. I could only see the tops of their heads and their shoulders but I knew that they were smiling. And there was such hope coming off them that I felt it too. I didn't worry. I tried with the back of my brain to find all of the things that had consumed me, kept me feeling over and apart, but they weren't there. I could remember them but not feel them. And there was music too. The movements on my back. The tune, the tune. I knew it but I couldn't find the name. It didn't matter, though. It didn't matter.

Everything was very warm and bright, through the little hole and how was it so bright what time was it where was I. I wanted one of them to look up, and be me. Just me, but older. But they never did, and soon I felt the little movements cease. By the time I had the energy to stand up, I couldn't tell if anything had been there or if my brain was playing a sort of trick on me. My head ached and my stomach felt heavy. I was thirsty, but the thought of putting anything at all into my body felt too much. It was morning and my jeans were dusty and stained with creamy bile. My nice top had ridden up over my bra and one of my breasts had popped out. I tucked it in and rearranged myself. The pigeons in the rafters were moving and slants of light were breaking through the roof. Pale and golden. I ran my fingers through my hair and picked out a desiccated leaf.

Nadia and Cian had gone – back to bed, I assumed. I looked downstairs for my phone and couldn't find it. Picked up a sleeping bag from the corner of the room to carry back. It was bulky and electric blue outside and bright pink inside. It had been Dad's and I had used it on the first sleepover that I ever went on. The floor of the room was littered with cans and cigarette butts. Paul Shee-han from the rowing team had been there, I remembered, and Meadhbh Fahy, who was in fourth year and had an undercut. Everyone had seen me at my worst. The haw-thorn trees were fat with thick white blossoms. I hoped nobody had recorded it. I didn't want the world to see me raw and foolish. I didn't want to have to be ashamed.

I remembered the ghost story Nadia had told me, about the woman and the daughter and the baby who had been so powerless and then so brutal. And when I got back home, the house was quiet, and Cian had left the back door unlocked for me. I remembered all the things he'd said. I changed into my blue Penneys pyjamas and clam-bered into bed. Later when I showered, there were marks on my body I couldn't explain and didn't want to think about. Bruises and scrapes, and four small circular burns arranged in a rectangular fashion, that only stung when I discovered them.

Missing in the Morning

Leontia huddled with the others on the side of the road, waiting for the minibus that would bring them to the one pub in the lonely place out in the country where they were staying for the weekend. It was Kate's parents' holiday home, halfway past nowhere, and they were supposed to be working on a play for the student drama festival. Muireann had written it, in the wake of a bad break-up, and Brian was directing. Leontia had never been in a play before, not properly. She'd always ended up in the background, an orphan or a singing nun. In the nativities at primary school, she'd been livestock seven years in a row. But that was a long time ago and she was eighteen now, and in college. She had friends and she was in a play.

Her dad had been so happy, dropping her off. He'd always said to her, when she was having arguments with the girls, or feeling low, that some people find themselves in college and that's just how it is and that it had been that way for him, back in the day. He told Leontia that she was more like her old dad than she realized, and she felt the sting of that, the truth in it. Her dad was a nice man, but a little awkward. There was a hopeful, lost sort of look about him always. He wanted to be better to people than they were to him, but sometimes it frustrated him and he

167

would snap at her or her mother. Leontia remembered
looking at his polka-dot shirt underneath the cashmere
v-neck jumper her mother had bought him for Christmas, and wishing he would hurry up and drive instead
of trying to parent her when he wasn't any good at it. She
held her tongue and smiled at him and thanked him, swallowing annoyance down, and nerves.

Kate was tall and thin. She was in recovery from an
eating disorder and always talking about it. She went to
therapy twice a week and she was bisexual. Important
things happened to Kate. She was complex like a character
in a film or a play, not like a real person. Leontia wasn't a
real person either, but in a different way. She misted in and
misted out of life. She had several groups of friends, and
felt inessential to each of them. But Kate was a key part of
the food chain or ecosystem or whatever strange thing the
drama society was, and Leontia had long red curly hair
like Muireann's ex-girlfriend Mary and could do a good
impression of someone worried or sad. When she was
kissing Kate during rehearsals, Leontia felt something in
the pit of her stomach a bit like fear that she didn't want to
look at too closely.

Brian was a second-year Philosophy student and was
always going on about phenomenology but Leontia couldn't
get her head around what that was or why it was so interesting. He wore black cotton shirts and black trousers and
looked like someone who worked in Dunnes only without
the name tag. This was the second play he'd directed. He'd
done a one-act by John B. Keane last year which had gone
down well and so it had the ring of authority when he said:
kiss her harder, wrap your hand around her waist and put
your other hand just under her armpit Kate are you okay if
she touches your breast a little would that work.

The minibus was run by local people, volunteers. Tonight, it was being driven by a man called Mikeen who apparently did bus tours for Americans when there were any. Having a minibus to the pub was supposed to stop rural isolation and drink driving. You put two euro in for the petrol, and bought Mikeen a Lucozade if he didn't have a drink in front of him. Mikeen was a well-groomed man with very clean hands. He looked like the principal of a school or an accountant, not a rural bus tour man. Though, Leontia supposed she didn't really know what a rural bus tour man was supposed to look like.

Muireann sat beside Leontia and they didn't speak for the entire bus ride. Leontia felt questions rising in her mouth, but none of them felt right or good enough and so she swallowed them down rather than say something wrong about the mountains looking like someone had torn the bottom of a piece of pink and grey paper and left a sort of dark void poking through and how she hoped the stars would soon arrive. There were a few other people on the bus, older men mostly. Some of them looked dirty, with suit jackets over acrylic jumpers and flat caps and either a tan or dirt. Some were like Mikeen, tidy and unassuming. Kate nodded to them and sometimes they asked whose girl she was and nodded when she told them and asked how her parents were getting on. Brian smiled at them and played with his earlobe. He always did that, and it looked like he was deep in thought but maybe it was just something he did without realizing. Leontia chewed her pens and sometimes she'd just space out and suddenly taste ink inside her mouth and feel ashamed. She didn't like taking out a pen that had been chewed to bits but she didn't want to throw out a pen that still worked either, so she mainly took notes on her laptop now. Leontia's parents had bought it for her when she turned seventeen, the year that she refused to go to school, to try and convince her that they were on her side. It didn't work.

'I wonder what Tara and Joe are up to,' said Kate, and Muireann crooked a smile at her. Tara and Joe were a couple who had gotten together in September and were basically married now. They went everywhere together, and were talking about living together next year, if they could find a place. They had been to Kate's parents' house before when they were all in that John B. Keane one-act that everyone was always going on about, and had asked to come along, even though Joe wasn't even in the play this time.

Leontia felt a little thing between her teeth, a rib of something, and tried to get it out with her tongue in a subtle way. She didn't want to be seen to be picking her teeth. She didn't want to be a person with an imperfect and disgusting body in front of the drama crowd, and particularly in front of Kate, who could roll her hair up into a perfect messy twist on the top of her head and make it look effortless. Kate was laughing at something one of the aul lads had said and Brian was rolling a cigarette. Brian rolled his own cigarettes, and Muireann had said to Leontia that of course he did and Leontia had laughed as though she knew what that meant but it had puzzled her, and later on she'd wondered if it was something about drugs. Leontia's mother was always warning her about people offering her drugs or trying to rape her and so far nobody had done either of those things and she mostly felt relieved about it, but sometimes she wondered if life was passing her by.

The minibus pulled up to a small pub, the size of a dormer bungalow with a dark brown porch. It looked like it was made out of the same stuff that the lawn furniture Leontia's parents owned was, the kind that had been stained a dark, rich colour but gotten paler and patchier over the years, not just because Leontia's dad kept forgetting to bring it in at night (which Leontia's mother had decided was his job), but because they were cheap and even if you take care of cheap things they'll fall apart eventually. The garden furniture at the back of Kate's parents' cottage was thick plastic, but not the white kind that cracked – the thick kind that looked like it had been designed by someone, which it had. When Leontia had said she liked it, Kate had smiled and said two names to her that she didn't know and couldn't remember now. The pub smelled like cigarettes and spilt beer, and Tara and Joe were probably at it back at the house. There weren't very many people there, maybe nine others: two women deep in talk, a huddled back of indeterminate gender, the barman, and a group of five with musical instruments beside them.

'Will there be music?' asked Brian, and Kate said maybe. If they felt like it they'd probably start. Leontia didn't like trad music. It reminded her of family gatherings where relatives hugged her too tightly on the stairs and cried about things she didn't understand. After one such gathering her mother had vomited in the dog's basket and made Leontia clean it up the next day, as if a stranger had done it. Leontia had been more disgusted by the thought that her mother could drink enough to vomit than by the stuff itself, which had been pale and full of small pieces of meringue.

It seemed like a very teenage thing for an adult to do, and cleaning it up seemed like a very adult thing for a teenager to be asked to do, and it unbalanced her. She had never referred to it, and neither had her mother. That was the way things were with them in general, so it had come as a bit of a surprise when her father hadn't got the hint and had taken digs at his wife the whole next week until she started to cry into her lasagne and tell him that he never let things go and she was sorry but she hadn't eaten because she was too busy cleaning the house to get ready for the party and not one of them had lifted a fucking finger to help her and it was always the way with him to stand back and let other people do everything and then pick on them when they made one mistake.

Leontia hadn't known what to do – maybe if Steven had been there, they could have rolled their eyes at each other and softened it or something, but there was no one else and so she'd quietly taken her plate and two large slices of garlic bread to her room and posted a picture of them because one of the slices of garlic bread looked a bit like it had a face on it. Three people had liked it and no one had commented, and in the morning her parents had been okay with each other again, but both of them had been really frosty to her and made snide remarks about 'eating as a family' and 'the food we put on your plate' and it had been confusing but there didn't seem to be a right way for Leontia to be in the world and she was thinking about her parents too much when she was supposed to be here, making new friends and being someone better than she was.

'What are you drinking?' asked Kate and Leontia said she'd go up with her and have a look because she couldn't afford to be buying drink for people and didn't want the awkwardness of looking at the level of Kate's glass and waiting to ask her if she wanted the same again and then maybe someone else would want her to get them a drink and she only had fifty euro in her wallet and it had to do her until she got home.

Kate ordered a red wine and a pint of cider for Muireann. Leontia got a vodka and white because it was the drink she had the most experience with, and she could gauge how drunk she'd be after three of them pretty well. Brian ordered a Coke, but took it to the bathroom and Kate said he had whiskey in his bag. Her tone was neutral, and Leontia couldn't get a read on whether that was acceptable behaviour or not, in this pub where they stuck out so much with their clothes and youth and accents. They'd had a good rehearsal earlier, and Muireann explained to them what the scene was about, and where Mary had been coming from and how Muireann hadn't meant to hurt her, but had anyway. Brian disagreed with Muireann about the scene, and thought that she was being too soft on Mary, who had pecked away at her like a crow. He had suggested in an earlier rehearsal that Kate might hit Leontia, and that Leontia might deserve it, and they had demurred, but he told them that he 'really wanted to try it that way tomorrow' and that it would 'add something, wouldn't it?'

He looked at Leontia as though she could make the decision, but Muireann interrupted that it wasn't how it happened, and Brian said he knew that and he knew that hitting women wasn't okay, but for the sake of making it more theatrical, of giving the audience some *moment* that would move and shock them, that it could be justified.

'I don't want anybody thinking I was abusive to her,' said Muireann. 'I didn't mean for it to be like this. For us to be a story. I just wanted to explain it to myself.'

And Kate rubbed her back and told her that she understood, she got it.

And Leontia wondered if she was going to spend tomorrow being slapped in the face over and over again, while Brian nodded and made notes in his little book that Kate had called 'a knock-off Moleskine' as though not paying twenty euro for a copybook was something that a person should be ashamed of. Leontia looked down at her fleece-lined Penneys boots and reminded herself that she was as good as any of them. It wasn't her fault that she had fewer opinions. She sipped her drink, trying to make it last.

An old man in the corner began to sing, and people quieted down, though it had been quiet anyway. There was a woman beside him with an accordion and another, older woman with a bodhrán. One of the old men from the minibus strummed on a guitar and Leontia wondered if it was going to be a session, and if it would be loud, and if Kate and Muireann were going to hook up and if Brian would be hurt by that, because he kept making excuses to touch Kate when he was directing scenes, and she'd told Leontia that it would be creepy coming from someone else but that there was something helpless about him. Leontia hadn't noticed Brian touching Kate until she'd said, and then she saw it all the time. His hand on her chin, tilting her head up and explaining how she needed to stand there and catch the light in a scene for it to make more of an impact. He cared more about how things looked than how they sounded, and she wondered if that was the way to do it, because she wanted the words to sound right inside her mouth. Natural. She'd never had a girlfriend, or a boyfriend. And she wanted on the stage to look like someone who had, and did and could. She wanted to be able to give Kate as good as she got.

The song was about running water, and the water was the sea or maybe tears. Probably the sea though, old songs tended to be about the sea, and the chorus had a line they kept repeating over and over again, *One of us was missing in the morning*, and it made her feel uncomfortable, because she thought about Steven and the caravan park they had gone to when she was six and what had happened there, even though it hadn't been the sea but just a lake. It had done the job though, probably.

Muireann was drinking a pint of Guinness now and rolling her eyes at almost everything Brian said, so Leontia asked her about costumes to try and calm things down. Muireann said that was Tara's deal, but she still had some of Mary's clothes, and Mary had said she didn't want them back so they might as well use them. She asked Leontia what size she was and Leontia told her, and knew from Muireann's face that she was bigger than Mary. But couldn't Muireann have told that with her eyes without making her say numbers in front of people in a pub, but people don't think sometimes, and if Tara had to do some alterations it was probably important that they know. Leontia asked Muireann if she missed Mary and she said she did, and that she thought writing a play about the demise of their relationship would help her to process what had happened and move on, but it was having the opposite effect, really.

Muireann drained her pint and went up to the bar and slapped another vodka and white down in front of Leontia and smiled. Leontia smiled back and felt sick to her stomach at the thought of getting into rounds and then not having any money for the rest of the weekend. There was nothing on her debit card but maybe she could ring her mother and ask her to transfer something, and maybe if she did it right this minute it would be there the following morning.

One of us was missing in the morning.

Steven didn't have a room in their house. You hear of people keeping a dead child's room like a museum, but that's in houses where they have the space. The two of them had shared, and Leontia was in that room now, the one that had been theirs and was now hers. It was nice to have that privacy. She wondered what would have happened if he'd lived. A teenage girl and a teenage boy shouldn't share a room, there was something off about that. But they had the house they had, and maybe she would just have been the weird girl who shared a room with her brother, instead of the quiet girl in the back. No one really knew about Steven. She didn't talk about him, but not because she couldn't put words on it. It wasn't complicated, what had happened. But he had been the centre of attention in life, as in death, and she didn't want the most interesting thing about her to be a story about someone else.

Her parents had been in the little ramshackle pub down the road, not unlike this one. And they'd left her with Steven, because she was six and he was four and a great little sleeper. A great little everything. Her job had been to keep an eye on him. Her mother said later: 'I don't wish that it had been you, but I wish it hadn't been him.' People had asked her over and over again what had happened. Leontia didn't know. She had half-heard him saying he was going to 'out to see' something, but she'd been drifting in and out of sleep. Everyone said it wasn't her fault and she was only a child, but she was old enough to know it wasn't safe for him to go outside in the dark. She hadn't thought of it in terms of him getting hurt, but only a sort of smugness at the trouble he'd be in with Mammy and Daddy when they came back. She had seen him open up the door, and she had turned her back and closed her eyes.

The woman was singing now, another song that felt old and new at once. Her voice was high and clear, and everyone put their drink down. The phrase she kept repeating in the chorus was *the night you tried to die*, and that was strange as well, because of that time in fifth year when Leontia had taken nineteen Panadol and ended up vomiting them into the kitchen sink. It had been three in the morning and she hadn't been able to sleep and she'd had a pain in her head. She kept telling herself that if she could only ease it then maybe she would be able to think a little more clearly and make better choices. Or make choices at all. It was the sense of not even having a ticket to any of it, maybe. And the following day, with a raw throat and a banging in her temples, she had thought of him, his hand reaching out and opening the door. His small child's legs going out into the night. She hadn't thought of him when she was doing what she did. It was like her body was a puppet, and she was able to control it from outside herself, and look on clinically, thinking *that probably won't help but might as well*.

No one had known about it. It seemed stupid. It felt like it had happened in brackets. When people in shows tried to take their own lives, they used ropes, razors or interesting American drugs. The next day she went to school, and she told no one. There was a sense that nobody would care, that life would just continue on rails anyway. It could not be stopped. Her parents didn't know. Her friends didn't know. She hardly even admitted it to herself, or thought about it much. She had been frightened after, not about what could have happened, but about someone finding out. It was one thing to be sad, but another to be known to

be sad. There had been people in her year who had strug-
gled with that sort of thing, for various reasons, and it
hadn't gone well for them.

The song ended and everybody clapped. Leontia said
she was going up to the bar and did anyone want anything and she got glasses of Guinness for Kate and herself
and a whiskey for Brian. Her money would be gone, she
realized. But that was fine. She'd find a way to cope. They
started singing about a woman who drank too much, and
she snorted, and Kate asked what the matter was and she
said nothing, thinking of her mother and the dog basket.
Kate started to tell her what the matter was with herself at
the moment, and how she was thinking of starting to put
some of her spoken word pieces on YouTube, to motivate
herself to write more, maybe turn it into a one-woman
show, and Leontia nodded wisely, as if she knew precisely
what the fuck Kate was on about. Kate ran her fingers
through her hair and it looked even better when she was
finished. Leontia sipped her glass of Guinness. It wasn't
nice, but that was fine. She'd make it last longer. Kate's
mouth was stained with wine and Leontia wanted not to
kiss her, but to put her thumb in the centre of her bottom
lip and feel how soft it was. She wanted to be close enough
to Kate that she could do that when she wasn't pretending
to be someone else.

She shook her head like a wet Old English sheepdog
and stood up to go to the bathroom. Brian looked at her as
she left, and she felt his eyes on her. If any of them stuck
around long enough, or got drunk enough, he would
probably make a move. And it would be weird afterwards,
but maybe it would also be a story people told. Proof that
she existed or something. She wasn't thinking clearly. Her
hands reached out and touched the white tile with the

black diamonds in the middle of it. They were smooth and cool. She was still here.

There was only one toilet and somebody was in it. She could hear them moving, and suddenly felt embarrassed, as if they were listening to her and not the other way around. She wasn't sure whether to stay or go, but she didn't want to have to get up again; they might think she was drunker than she was and she wasn't sure what they thought of that. Drinking was powerful but being drunk, or messy drunk, was not. She could see her own face in the mirror and none of her feelings were written on it. If it was just a picture of herself, she wouldn't know who she was or how she was by looking at it. The toilet flushed. It was the woman who had sung the song. Leontia moved around her and went into the cubicle. The woman didn't smile or shrug or speak or any of the other things that people generally do when they're moving around each other in a pub toilet. Leontia closed the door, and felt like she was locking it not for privacy, but against something else. She sat on the seat and breathed in and out ten times before doing what she was there to do. She didn't want to take too long in case they noticed and made jokes. Jokes made her uncomfortable. She was never sure if she should laugh along or be offended, and couldn't seem to get the balance right. She wished people came with subtitles. She'd still miss things, but maybe less so.

She washed her hands with the horrible pink soap that smelled like cheap detergent, looked at the choice of wet towel or filthy-looking hand dryer, deciding instead to dry them on her bag. It only kind of worked. But they were mostly dry and nobody was going to shake her hand, they weren't politicians or business-lads.

Kate and Brian were sitting closer together when she returned, and Muireann had gone outside to have a smoke. Leontia listened to the two of them talking and tried to find enough to say so she wasn't just sitting beside them listening like a note-taker. She checked her phone. The only messages she had were from her dad. She told him they were in the pub, and that it was fun. He'd like that. Her in the pub having fun with people.

He replied to remind her not to mix drinks. Leontia's father seemed to think that if you had a beer, a wine and a vodka on the same night you would surely end up in the accident and emergency department. Or worse. Or worse meant sex she supposed. There wasn't any Wi-Fi, which was annoying. Kate's house had it, but Kate's house would. When she kissed Kate, her mouth tasted like cinnamon toothpaste or filter coffee. Leontia didn't like either of those things but the idea of them was something. Most people she had kissed just tasted like breath, and tongue.

Steven would be fifteen now, if he had lived. And maybe he had lived. Her mother said once that maybe he had been found by people who wanted a little boy and couldn't have one. And maybe he grew up with them, having everything he needed and being loved. Leontia didn't think that could have happened. She thought he'd drowned but they had dragged the lake and couldn't find him. Which didn't mean he wasn't there. Lakes are big and dark, and full of places little things could hide. His chubby hand on the door. Leontia rose, gathered up her bag, and said 'excuse me'. She walked out on the porch. Muireann was sitting, looking at an ashtray.

'I miss her so much,' she said.

Leontia said 'I know you do', and looked out at the darkness. There were no lights beyond the ones coming from the pub itself; she could see across the road but after that it all pooled into one. She craned her head right back and saw the stars, so clear you could play dot-to-dot with them. Leontia shivered. It was cold. Muireann put an arm around her and Leontia put her head on Muireann's shoulder. Underneath the layers of cloth and skin, she could feel their rib cages against each other, side by side.

'Are you not cold?' she asked. 'You're only wearing a t-shirt out here in the dark.'

She could feel Muireann smile.

'Can I have a cigarette?' she asked.

'You don't smoke,' Muireann said, and Leontia said she knew but that she wanted to do something with her hands, and so Muireann gave her a cigarette, and cupped her hands to help her use the flame.

'Have you ever had a broken heart?' she asked. And Leontia nodded slowly, though she hadn't. Not in the way that Muireann seemed to mean.

'It's *horrible*.' Muireann's face was strange, half in shadow, parts all lit up wrong like oil on water. 'I know I keep going on about Mary, and that I wrote the whole play about Mary, and there are times I wish I could just kick her out of my head but at the same time she's the only thing I want to talk about. When other people say things to me, I'm waiting for my turn so I can bring her up.'

'That's a lot,' Leontia said.

'She messaged me about the play, you know. Asked me not to do it. And I'm doing it anyway and I didn't even change the names and she called me abusive and I don't know, maybe I am. I mean all of our friends will come to it and they'll see a version of it I made up.'

'It's not the exact same though,' Leontia said.

'It's pretty close.'

'You kill her at the end.'

'I didn't mean to.'

Leontia nodded, remembering the times she had seen Mary in passing, in the canteen or wandering through the Arts Block. She'd looked very much alive. Always wearing a tweedy-looking jacket and holding a KeepCup full of – according to the play – Valerian root tea. Leontia had been on her social media as research and it was updated pretty regularly. She was definitely a girl and not a ghost.

Leontia stared at Muireann, at the tilt of her neck and the sureness of her body in its oversized top. She felt the smoke hit the back of her throat and she swallowed down a little cough. It pooled in the air like a cloud and it made the night look like something she had a little bit of control over. Brian came out holding everyone's coats and bags, and with some of Kate's lipstick on his face. Kate was behind him and she looked immaculate.

'It's still going on in there,' she said, 'but I kind of want to head back home and Mikeen says he'll drop us back for thirty euro.'

Music was drifting out again, out into the dark of the night, filling quiet places. Mikeen said they could smoke inside the bus, half of the aul lads did anyway, but the two of them stubbed out their cigarettes and followed Kate and Brian, still carrying everyone's things, and the bus drove back towards Kate's parents' house, where Joe and Tara were. Leontia was quiet looking out into the velvet dark, thinking of the nettles and the dock leaves, the hawthorn and wild garlic, the sheep and cows and donkeys and the animals she hadn't seen at all – the wild ones, like the badgers and the foxes. Every big and little thing out there inside the quiet. And what would it be like to turn the handle on a door, and just go out to see, and not come back. She felt a strange stretching in her, a sort of longing to move her legs as far and as fast into the night as they would go. And she knew that if she decided it was what she was going to do, that none of them could stop her. She was too strong, too big. They wouldn't dare.

Acknowledgements

This book wouldn't have come together if Claire Hennessy, Eimear Ryan and Laura Cassidy hadn't supported and believed in my short fiction. Their faith, insight and warmth since the very first story I had published in *Banshee* has been deeply appreciated and I'm delighted we got to take this journey together.

Anna Morrison designed the beautiful cover, and I'm quite happy for the book to get judged by it to be honest. Thanks so much Anna.

My agent, Clare Wallace and all the team at Darley Anderson are tireless champions of my work and it's a privilege to have them in my corner.

Several of these stories have been published in other places. Sending a new piece of work out into the world can be daunting and I'm very grateful in particular to Brendan Barrington of *The Dublin Review*, Sinéad Gleeson, who kindly included 'Black Spot' in *The Art of the Glimpse* anthology, Marc O'Connell and Cethan Leahy of *The Penny Dreadful*, Kathy D'Arcy who edited the *Autonomy* anthology, and Brian J. Showers of Swan River Press for welcoming my work and for their editorial feedback.

I was first published because of the faith and support of another writer, Siobhán Parkinson, and since then I've been lucky enough to encounter so much kindness. In terms of my short stories, Nuala O'Connor was complimentary about a piece of flash fiction I wrote and even though it's not included in this book, her words kept me going as I worked on the stories that are. Marian Keyes, Louise O'Neill, Tara Flynn, Lucy Sweeney Byrne and Danielle McLaughlin have all taken the time to read and respond to this book, and their generosity is deeply appreciated.

Kennys Bookshop is a Galway institution, and their belief in *I Want to Know That I Will Be Okay* has been such a boost. Des, Tom, Tomás and Sarah, go raibh míle maith agaibh.

Sarah Maria Griffin, Sarah Davis-Goff and Dave Rudden, for chats, encouragement and general soundness.

Maria Griffin, Suzanne Keaveney and Ciara Banks for checking in and being class.

Mam, Dad, Tadhg and Cam, and my extended family, in particular my late Uncle Brian, for their support of my work.

And finally, Diarmuid, Bonnie and Arthur. My home. My heart. My cat.

BANSHEE
PRESS

Banshee Press was founded by writers Laura Cassidy, Claire Hennessy and Eimear Ryan. Since 2015, they have published *Banshee* literary journal twice a year. The Banshee Press publishing imprint launched in 2019. Titles include *Paris Syndrome* by Lucy Sweeney Byrne and *Gold Light Shining* by Bebe Ashley.

WWW.BANSHEELIT.COM